GENESIS

"It's crazy up there." Kingston grabs the gun strapped to his shoulder. He checks to see how many bullets are left in the magazine. "They've got the place completely surrounded and we're almost out of ammo. The other gun's out and this magazine's practically empty."

The gunfire above us ceases, pulling everyone's eyes to the ceiling. A low whistle replaces the sound, quickly crescendoing in volume.

"What is that?" Ria questions. Like everyone else, her gaze is fixed on the hole in the ceiling.

Boom!

"Watch out!" I tackle my brother out of the way.

A bright light rips through the center of the vehicle and levitates the battered military truck at least ten feet into the air. A blaze of fire shoots down through the open manhole, illuminating our surroundings for a few seconds before the truck comes crashing back down onto the street.

Rollins releases a deep moan and rolls onto his back. He tries to push me off of him, but he doesn't have the strength. The fire dissipates, leaving the underground room unharmed.

"Good Lord, what was that?"

Everyone lays scattered across the floor.

"I think they just dropped a bomb on us," Kingston coughs.

1

OTHER BOOKS BY R.L. MCDANIEL

The Big Hoot

Levitation Series (Book 1)

Levitation: Genesis

Book 2

R.L. McDaniel

For Joe,

who has always treated me more like a brother

CHAPTER 1

TRAIN STATION

"We're just wasting time," my older brother says as he stares up at the MagneTrain arrivals' board. The subsectors are listed in alphabetical order on the digital screen along with the time each train should arrive at this station. Every few minutes the board is updated, flashing a time change for an incoming arrival. "How do we even know the message was for us?"

The image of a peculiar sentence I spotted earlier on the downtown Jumbotron, nicknamed The Beacon, pops back in my head. It could have been a glitch or simply a coincidence, but something in my gut tells me it was meant for us since we have no way of communicating by Receiver. At the exact moment I glanced up at the enormous screen, a message flitted across for a split second interrupting the normal broadcast of the loop of Government-controlled news:

———

Train Station 9 AM

———

"Or it could be a trap," Kingston warns as he approaches with Ria after doing a sweep of the train station.

"We didn't see anything but FootSoldiers crawling all over the place." Ria runs her fingers through her recently cut hair. Her pink bangs are gone, but a blonde fringe still frames her face. She snakes her hand through my elbow and pulls me closer. "Even in these disguises, they can still scan us. We probably should keep moving."

"Can't scan us without Receivers," Rollins says low to the group. He takes his eyes off the board for the first time since we arrived. He removes his fake prescription glasses and scratches at the side of his nose; his jacket sleeve slides up to reveal the tracking device usually around his wrist is missing.

Our Receivers—the devices everyone receives as a birthday present from the Government when they turn seven—were removed from our wrists when we were sent to the Compound. In its place, a chip was surgically implanted into the backs of our necks giving the Government the ability to control our minds. Luckily, thanks to the virus that Ren installed, the chips are now nothing more than a benign piece of metal and plastic in our heads.

I pull my sweatshirt hood back over the top of my recently shaved head and scan the room for security cameras for what seems like the hundredth time in the past five minutes. Other than the ones we dodged earlier when entering the train station, there don't seem to be any in the area.

Rollins glances back up at the arrivals board one more time just as a MagneTrain roars into the station and comes to a stop about twenty feet in front of us. The clock above the board reads 9:03 AM. The doors to each of the train cars open, allowing passengers to exit.

"It would help if we knew what we were looking for," I say, as I begin to scan individual faces, hoping that something tips me off to why we should be here.

8

One of the final passengers to exit the nearest train car is an older-looking man, possibly in his late forties or fifties with wild curly, gray hair. His eyes are small and his skin is darkened from the sun. He walks with a slight limp favoring his left side.

The man locks eyes with Rollins first, as if he recognizes him, before moving over to me and the rest of the group. He checks his surroundings before extracting a pre-war style hat from the inside of his jacket and places it on his head. He pulls the brim down low over his eyes but his gray locks still protrude from underneath.

I look over at Rollins. His gaze follows the man as he approaches us.

"Not here," the gray-haired man says as he passes us. He now refuses to make eye contact with anyone. His eyes study the ground as he continues down to the opposite end of the train station and takes a seat on an empty bench. An exit sign is posted on a wall above where he sits. He carefully places his briefcase next to him with the handle facing up. An additional bench remains unoccupied behind him.

We take a seat behind the man, so our backs are facing his, and he begins to talk.

"We don't have a lot of time," the man says in a slightly hoarse voice. He clears his throat before continuing. "My name is Dr. Max Dreadnought. I used to work with your father in the lab."

"Dad didn't work in a lab," I interrupt the man, correcting him. I begin to turn toward the doctor before I am able to catch myself. "He was a computer guy for Sol. He fixed computers." I look at Rollins for support.

"There's a lot that you don't know about your father." Dreadnought pauses for a second as his eyes find a pair of FootSoldiers marching across the open station floor heading in our direction. He pulls his hat's brim even farther down over his eyes and ducks his head. "I shouldn't have come here."

9

The doctor abruptly ends the short conversation by getting up. The briefcase remains on the bench where he originally placed it.

"Wait!" I call out in a panic. I stand, turning around toward the man. "What are we—" Rollins grabs my hand and yanks me back down to the bench, silencing me.

"There's a file in the briefcase that you need to see. Look it over. Memorize it." The man glances over at the approaching FootSoldiers one more time. The dark, metallic drones robotically march their way across the floor ordering the crowd to part. Their sights are set on the gray-haired doctor who is standing behind us. "My son was at the Compound with you. If anything, please end this madness for him."

"Your son?" Kingston asks confused.

"I've already said too much…stayed too long." Dreadnought's eyes skittishly shift from the approaching pair of FootSoldiers to his right to the closest exit where a group of three FootSoldiers just entered. All five drones raise their guns to their chests, silently ordering the crowd before them to disperse. Their eyes glow a sinister red, instantly scanning individuals as they pass. This is not a routine check; they're looking for someone in particular.

A gun goes off behind us causing the crowd of people in the station to scream and drop to the floor, including the four of us. I spot Dreadnought holding a pistol in his hand, erratically firing more rounds into the air. Each time he squeezes the trigger his hand flinches, shooting the bullets off at an unusual angle.

In all of the commotion, a confused woman cries as she cradles a child tightly in her arms down on the floor about ten feet away. Dreadnought glances over at the yelling woman for a second then back at us. He flashes us a panicked look before taking off toward another exit in the opposite direction. He waves his gun around in front of him, threatening people to get out of his way.

"Come on," Rollins shouts over all the screaming, "we've gotta get out of here!"

I push myself up off the floor and grab Dreadnought's briefcase from the bench behind us. Staying low, the four of us sprint toward an open train that is getting ready to depart the station. As we reach the platform, another set of gunshots erupts in the crowd followed by more screams behind us.

We jump into the train car just as the doors close, sealing us in. The MagneTrain, supported and powered solely by magnets, begins to push off toward its unknown destination, carrying us away from the station and all of the chaos.

CHAPTER 2

MISSING RECEIVERS

"The first thing we have to do is find something that will play this," Rollins says to the group. He shows us a flash drive about the size of a pinky nail in the palm of his hand. "You sure there's nothing else in there?"

I recheck all of the pockets and compartments in the briefcase for at least the tenth time since originally opening it. I shake my head. "Still empty."

"The one time we actually need a Receiver, we don't have one," Ria says, exhaling loudly through her nose. She glances around the half-filled train car. "It's too bad we can't just borrow someone's for a few minutes."

"Maybe we can," Kingston says. He eyes two attractive teenage girls sitting across the aisle. Both girls, who look maybe fifteen or sixteen years old, are neatly dressed in matching school uniforms—green and blue plaid skirts with white button-up blouses. They have their hair braided; one blonde and the other brunette. "Must be private school girls," he says under his breath, giving them a wink. "They're dumber than dirt."

The blonde sitting closer to us immediately turns away and releases a high-pitch giggle, burying her face into her huddled friend's shoulder. She quickly recovers and steals another glance over at Kingston, giving him a flirtatious smile.

Kingston nods his head back in their direction. "Hey girls, how's it going?" He confidently raises the side of his mouth and flashes a smooth, wry grin in their direction. One of his front upper teeth is missing, probably from the recent battle in the Arena.

The blonde leans in from across the aisle with a smile. "We were just saying how hot your accent is." She begins to lose her composure and turns away to bury her face into her friend's shoulder again with another giggle.

"I can't believe you just said that," the brunette says loud enough for all of us to clearly hear between laughs. She covers her mouth with the side of her hand. "You don't even know him! He could be a creeper." Her voice rises to a squeak as she finishes the sentence.

"I can promise you both, I am no such thing," Kingston says. He gets up and walks across the aisle, plopping himself down in one of the two open seats facing the girls. Rollins joins him and sits across from the brunette.

"So, what's your name?" Kingston asks the blonde. His eyes shoot down to her wrist and find her Receiver. Kingston grabs at his empty wrist, massaging it where his own device was once fastened.

"She's Kira," the brunette answers for her with a straight look on her face. "And I'm Eva."

The outside blurred scenery begins to take shape as the MagneTrain begins to decrease in speed. We must be approaching the next station.

"And this is my buddy, Rollins," Kingston says. He lightly slaps the side of my brother's arm next to him. He glances out the window, probably realizing that he needs to work fast before turning back to the girls. "Now that we know each other a little better, what do you say—"

"Citizens of Sol," an electronic-sounding voice comes on over the speakers in the ceiling and interrupts Kingston. "We ask that you stay in your seat and have your Receiver available when a FootSoldier approaches you. Please close out any active programs and remove any garments that may be covering the device that could slow down the scanning process. We apologize for any inconvenience this may cause. Thank you for choosing Sol's MagneTrain Services for all of your transportation needs, where your safety is our top priority."

As soon as the announcement is complete, the door in the front of our train car slides open and deposits two FootSoldiers. Both drones stand at attention, as if guarding the open door until it slides shut behind them. The Soldiers stiffly move forward, both holding some sort of thin black rod about the length of my arm with a glowing blue tip. Each Soldier takes one side of the aisle and scans passengers' Receivers in a systematic manner, starting from the front and working its way to the back where we all sit.

Kingston timidly glances over his shoulder and eyes the drones ten or twelve rows away. He whispers something to Rollins before returning his attention to the girls. Their entire demeanor has now changed as they sit straight up with tense expressions. One of the girls bites nervously at her nails.

"Everything okay?" Rollins asks, also reading the sudden change in their body language. He raises an eyebrow. The train comes to a stop, but the doors to our left and right remain closed.

"Yeah," Kira says. She stares out the window at the people standing on the platform waiting to get on the arriving train. "This is our stop. We need to get to school. We've already been late twice this week." She shoots a look over to Eva, but her friend's attention is somewhere else completely; her eyes are glued to the back of the closest FootSoldier as it completes another scan.

Eva bends over and grabs the backpack at her feet, clutching it in her arms. She apprehensively looks around the seats in front of her and studies the FootSoldiers. Her eyes dart all around the train car, looking for what I can only assume is a way out. She's gonna make a break for it.

I glance back at the closed door to my left—the closest exit. I have to do something before this girl gets us caught.

Careful to not make any sudden movements, I slide the briefcase over to Ria. "I think I have an idea, but I'll need a distraction. When I give you the signal, send this flying."

Ria glances down at the case and nods her head. Her eyes dart to the front of the train car, moving back and forth between the two FootSoldiers.

I wait until both drones begin their next scan, something I know can take anywhere from a few seconds up to a minute to complete. I open the palm of my hand, concealing it the best I can behind the seat in front of me, and aim it toward the closed set of doors to my left. I concentrate solely on the middle, where the two doors join together, and block everything else out around me.

The doors hold together for maybe ten seconds before giving way to my telekinesis, and begin to part to the sides. A strong gust of warm wind blows into the interior of the train car.

"Now!" I yell, giving the signal.

Before I can even get out of my seat, Ria sends Dreadnought's briefcase flying toward the front of the car. It strikes the luggage rack just above one of the drones' heads, causing a handful of bags to fall down onto the drone.

The two schoolgirls take the opportunity and dash out through the exit I created, while incoming passengers attempt to board through the one open door. Kingston and Rollins follow them, with Ria and myself immediately on their heels.

A single blue streak of light flashes by the side of my face and burns a hole through the doorframe of the exit door. An image of the FootSoldier's deadly weapon flashes through my head.

I watch as the girls scurry up a long set of stairs that leads out to the shady streets of a subsector of Sol that none of us have ever been to, or ever cared to visit.

CHAPTER 3

SRUNE

As soon as we reach the top of the staircase, we watch as the girls scamper across the street. They dodge moving vehicles left and right, and enter a ramshackle apartment building located across from the MagneTrain entrance.

"Now what?" I question the group. I spot a graffiti-filled sign posted at the top of the stairs with *Srune* painted in bold letters. Large abandoned buildings, most only partially intact, line both sides of the street illustrating a melancholy post-war picture we've become so accustomed to.

No one says a word. A gun goes off down the street that breaks the silence, followed by a woman's scream and the sound of glass breaking.

"We can't just stay here!" I look back down the staircase and spot a small crowd beginning to grow. An arm suddenly juts from the crowd, pointing us out to the authorities. "Guys?" I back away from the top step.

"The way I see it, we still need a Receiver to play that thing, right? Rollins addresses the group, ignoring me. His eyes stay glued to the building across the road. "They're gonna expect us to run, not stay in the area."

Kingston nods his head. "Pretty smart thinking, mate."

"Our best chance is to use the girls," Rollins continues, motioning to the group. "Come on."

Rollins checks both sides of the trash-filled street before crossing. We follow him into the same dilapidated building the girls entered seconds ago. Once inside, we close the door and allow the darkness to engulf us in. The only light source seems to be the sun shining in through little slits in the wall all around the doorframe. I take a couple of steps forward, only to feel something large scurrying over my shoe. The animal squeaks out a sharp cry of dismay as its long tail slaps the inside part of my pants leg, upset that we've disrupted its home.

"Whoa! What was that?" I yell out, startled as I stumble backward. My deep voice echoes off the walls in what appears to be the lobby of an abandoned building.

"Oh, stop being a girl," Ria mocks me. She reaches out and grabs my hand. "It was probably just a rat or something."

Like that's supposed to make me feel better.

"Shhh...I think I found some stairs," Rollins says low under his breath. "I wonder if they're up there." His voice fades as he begins climbing the stairs in front of him. "Nic, you and—" he begins just as I see a glint of light reflect off something swinging through the air to strike him across the face.

Bam!

Rollins releases a muffled yelp and tumbles backward. His arms flail to the sides as he loses his balance, taking the rest of us out with him.

18

The object that made contact with his face drops to the ground and bounces off the floor with a metal-sounding *clink*.

"Stay away from us, you freaks!" a girl's voice shouts, followed by the front door opening. The sudden cascade of bright sunlight makes everything inside visible for a few seconds, including the two girls from the train as they escape. A short metal pipe lays on the floor a few feet away from where my brother lies unconscious.

Without thinking, I push myself up off the dirty floor and sprint out after them. A small crowd has gathered across the street at the stairwell's entrance to the MagneTrain. A single FootSoldier has its back to me, busily scanning people in the group. Its red, glowing eyes focus on the Receivers around the people's wrists. I hear a few conversations about a group of teen Teles who escaped the authorities on the train.

I look up the street just in time to spot the girls disappear around the corner of the building, cutting across the street that runs behind the apartments. I double back through the alley, hoping to surprise them at the next block.

Just as I turn the corner onto the next road—

BAM!

I slam into both girls, my force knocking all three of us to ground. The brunette, Eva, pushes herself up, and leaves her friend in the middle of the street to fend for herself. She hobbles off, clearly putting most of her weight on one ankle as she screams for help at the top of her lungs.

"Someone please! HELP ME!"

I flip myself over on my stomach and extend my hand out in front of me, aiming for the back of her shoe. Out of the corner of my eye, I see an elderly woman standing on her balcony a few floors up holding a large bucket in her arms.

19

The woman peers down at me, and then back toward Eva, who's about ten yards away. She dumps the contents of the bucket over the side of her balcony before going back inside her apartment, like everything she just witnessed was completely normal.

I focus my attention back on Eva. As soon as my force hits the back of her shoes, she flies forward. She tumbles down hard on the cement and lands on her stomach, painfully sliding forward a few feet.

She rolls over on her back and sits up, holding the side of her bloody arm. Both of her knees are scraped and bleeding.

"Please don't hurt me," she says with a shaky voice. "We were just messing around on the train. Please! We didn't know! We'll do whatever you want." She winces in pain but doesn't move.

I take my time pushing myself up and stand menacingly over the blonde, Kira, who seems to be just as shaken up as her friend. They now know what I am, and because of it, they both fear me.

This is going to be easier than I thought.

CHAPTER 4

ARRESTED

"We just need to use your Receiver for a few minutes," I say, eyeing Eva who is still sitting on the ground about fifteen yards away. A few other people from the neighborhood have come out on their balconies to watch our show, but none seem to be in too much of a hurry to call for help.

I turn toward Kira, who lies at my feet. Her eyes are busy studying my bare wrist where the end of my sweatshirt sleeve has scrunched up, leaving the area exposed.

"What happened to yours?" she questions from the ground. Her eyes finally look up and find mine.

I extend my arm out to help Kira up while her friend hobbles over to us in obvious pain. I glance back up at the backside of the building. Most of our spectators have given up, and have headed back into their apartments.

"Can't go into that now." I glance back and forth between them. "We have a file we need to play though, and no way to do it."

"None of you have Receivers?" Kira asks, not being able to comprehend my response. She's eyes my naked wrist again.

Feeling self-conscious, I pull the end of my sleeve back down over my hand and shake my head. "So you gonna help us or what?"

The girls look at each other, their eyes doing all of the communicating.

"Do we really have a choice in the matter?" Kira asks, not looking away from her friend.

* * *

When we get back to the apartment building, Rollins is conscious, but still sitting down on the floor. His back is leaning up against the wall as Ria kneels down by his side. Someone has left the door cracked-open, allowing a trail of light to partially illuminate the lobby of the building.

"How is he?" I question, staring down at my brother. His eyes seem out of focus and he has a reddish-pink mark stretching across his face. His nose looks swollen, but it's been broken countless times before from playing sports in school, so that's nothing new.

Rollins glares at the girls who stand timidly behind me. He doesn't know which one to blame for his current situation, so he scowls at them both.

"He'll be okay," Ria says, downplaying the situation. She looks back up at me, then over to the two girls.

"Sorry about your friend," Eva says with slight remorse in her voice. "We didn't know what else to do." She inches forward.

"Where's Kingston?" I glance up the staircase. A large spider web stretches across the walkway that leads halfway up to the first floor.

"He went out after you," Ria says. She lifts herself up and wipes her hands on the sides of her pants. "He didn't find you?"

I shake my head and turn back toward the door. "And there's a crowd forming across the street. I don't have to tell you who they're looking for."

The drab lobby grows silent for a few seconds. The sound of a rodent scurrying away into the hollow walls echoes behind me in the darkness.

"We'll find him," Rollins says. My brother grunts, as he pushes himself up off the floor. He gingerly touches the tip of his nose and squeezes his eyes shut. He grips the end of it between two fingers, and roughly straightens it out with one sharp yank. A bone-crunching crack emits from the center. Rollins rapidly shakes his head.

One of the two girls takes a step back toward the exit. Her shadow grows across the floor in the light.

"So," Eva says, with a slight tremble in her voice, "we have an idea on how you can get a Receiver."

"Yeah, we're just gonna use yours," Ria spits, as she moves closer into the light. The way the light reflects off only the bottom half of her face makes her appear more menacing than she really is.

"I'm assuming you need one that cannot be traced?" Kira says, as she steps forward, pretending she's not intimidated. She turns to her friend before looking back at the group. "Something that can't link you to the device?"

"If we use yours," Rollins says all matter-of-factly, "then they'll trace it back to you, not us." He wipes sweat off his forehead using the side of his shirt sleeve.

"What if we could get you a clean Receiver? One that doesn't belong to anyone," Eva jumps in. "That way, we can't be questioned later and *accidentally* say something that we shouldn't." She raises her eyebrows.

Rollins turns his back on the girls and positions himself in front of me and Ria. He lifts his own eyebrows and considers the idea. "Are these girls playing us?" he questions out of the corner of his mouth to no one in particular.

"We know someone who can alter them," Kira says hopefully. "We can take you to him."

Rollins's gaze shoots over to us and then back to the girls. "Fine, take us to your guy, but this better not be a setup."

"I'll grab Kingston," I say, as I turn toward the door. "You all stay here. It was getting pretty heated out there before."

Ria grabs my hand and pulls me back to her, placing a light kiss on my lips. She tilts her hand toward my cheek, and her breath gently tickles the outside edge of my ear as she whispers, "Be careful out there."

I nod my head and step outside of the cave-like building. The bright sunlight temporarily blinds me for a few seconds. The intense glare finally subsides in time for me to see the scene across the street has intensified. Multiple FootSoldiers have a crowd of at least twenty or thirty people lined up with their backs against the buildings on the other side of the street. A handful of citizens are lying face down on the sidewalk in front of the group, limbs handcuffed behind their backs.

I study the prisoners' faces as the majority of them squirm around, trying in vain to free their hands. One person, the only one positioned away from the road, is the calmest out of the group; possibly unconscious.

I creep up the street, heading up to the next block to get a better view of the crowd. I'm careful to camouflage myself behind a row of abandoned cars lined-up against the sidewalk. Could they have Kingston? Without a Receiver, they'll arrest him on the spot—it doesn't matter if they can identify him or not. It's illegal to be caught without the device.

I squint my eyes, as I halfway cross into the busy street. I spot a shaved head with a red ponytail sprouting out the back of it lying on its side.

Kingston.

They have Kingston.

CHAPTER 5

NOX

"This is all your fault!" Ria fumes, standing inches away from Eva's nose. She's backed her into a corner so she can't escape. "If it wasn't for that stunt you pulled earlier, Kingston would have never been out there in the first place."

I've never before heard such fierceness in Ria's voice. She trembles slightly, a scowl angrily molded across her face. She clenches a single fist down by her side as she waits for the girl to say something smart back. Her other hand, directed at the exit, telekinetically holds the door closed, keeping everyone inside.

"They're probably gonna take him to Processing and hold him there until they transfer him," Kira says, as she attempts to step in-between Ria and her friend. "We can show you where it is."

"And how do you expect us to get into Processing?" Rollins asks, sounding irritated. He touches the bridge of his swollen nose with his index finger. "Just stroll right in and inform them that we're there to pick up our friend?"

Ria doesn't budge. Her eyes are still focused on the girl in front of her.

"Our guy can get you in," Kira interjects, still trying to intervene between the two girls. "He can get you whatever you want."

"He better," Ria says, sounding somewhat satisfied. She takes a small step back and drops her hand. "Or you're gonna regret it."

* * *

We trek across Srune, taking as many back roads and alleys as possible, trying to keep ourselves off the grid to avoid the FootSoldiers who are still combing the streets searching for us. The Government will not rest until they have all four of us, and anyone else who escaped the Compound, behind bars.

My mind drifts to Ren and August. Did August ever find Ren? Did they make it out of the Compound alive? I glance over at Ria. She senses my stare, turning to me with a small smile as her eyes meet mine. One thing at a time, I tell myself.

We approach another apartment building in total shambles. It's not as bad as the one across from the MagneTrain entrance on the opposite side of the subsector, but it's nothing I'd ever imagine walking into in my previous life.

"Third floor," Eva says. She stares up at a random balcony on the side of the brick building. "Second door on the left."

Rollins turns toward our guides. "You're coming with us. We don't know what we're walking into up there."

Eva looks over at Kira and she shakes her head. "Fine. Just let us do the talking."

We enter the building from the front, only to find a rather obese man passed out, loudly snoring at the bottom of the staircase. He's halfway leaned up against the side of the railing so the top half of his unconscious body is still propped up. He holds an almost empty bottle of some kind of dark liquid in his meaty hand, resting it on his massive belly. Even sleeping, he cradles the bottle like a newborn baby in his arms, careful not to spill a drop.

We follow Eva and Kira carefully around the man and creep up the stairs. As we take each step, the staircase releases a moan. The rotten wood under our boots sounds like it's ready to give at any moment.

Once we reach the second floor, the wooden staircase seems to be a little stronger. No longer do I feel the wood warping beneath me if I stay on one step for too long.

We reach the third floor—second door on the left—just like Eva told us outside.

"Nox doesn't like me bringing new people around," Eva warns us for the first time, as we stand outside of the apartment. Music blares through the walls, thumping and vibrating the floor underneath. "He sort of has a crush on me, so if he starts to act weird, I'll meet you downstairs."

I glance over at Rollins and then Ria. Are these girls setting us up?

Eva looks over at Kira, before rapping at the door, loud enough so she can be heard over the music.

The door moves inward, already slightly cracked open. Eva pokes her head in. "Nox? You home?"

An older-looking teen, maybe eighteen or nineteen years old, sits in a recliner on the opposite end of a poorly lit room. He wears his greasy, jet black hair slicked back with the sides shaved down to his scalp. He's holding a wireless video game controller in his hand, yelling something incomprehensible through a headset to someone on the other end. He has on baggy clothes—his T-shirt and sweatpants seem to be at least a couple sizes too big.

"Boom! That's why you don't mess with the Nox-man!" the skinny teen shouts as he jumps out of his seat. He presses a button and shoots a pixelated military-looking character on the screen in the back of the head. His opponent's brains explode and splatter all over the television screen.

"Nox?" Eva calls out, this time even louder over the hip hop music blasting from the speakers. We stand inside the doorway of the apartment as he continues to play his video game.

Nox throws the controller down and beats his chest with closed fits. All of his attention is on the enormous television screen mounted on the wall. Dark red blood splatter from the recent headshot still stains the screen. He glances over, finally noticing all of us standing by the open door.

"Hey beautiful," Nox says. His eyes focus only on Eva. "I see you came to see the Nox-man." His eyes move away from Eva as he scrutinizes each of us. His demeanor instantly changes in front of our eyes. He leans over, lifting up a ballcap that rests on his recliner, and pulls a handgun out from underneath.

I grab Ria's hand, both of us taking a step back instinctively toward the door. My brother's eyes flash over to Eva.

Nox raises the gun and aims it at no one in particular. "Babygirl," he begins in a deep Southern accent, "you know you're welcome here anytime, but you know the rules."

The girl's mouth opens to speak.

"Eva, shut your mouth. It makes you look dumb when you leave it wide-open like that." He gracefully cocks back the hammer, ready to fire. "All I want to hear out of your pretty little mouth is one thing—why the hell you brought these fools up into my place."

29

CHAPTER 6

MONEY PROBLEMS

"Drones are looking for them," Eva says so quickly it's as if she had the statement ready on the tip of her tongue before entering the building.

Nox moves his gun over an inch so that Eva is in its sights. He squints his right eye and tilts his head to the side, scowling. He holds his stare for what feels like a full minute before finally lowering his gun. "You got money?" He nods at Rollins.

My brother sharply bobs his head once, before taking a few steps forward, away from the group. "I'm Rollins. We really apprec—"

"Did I ask you to talk?" Nox cuts him off, before stressing his name loudly in a mocking tone, "*Raw-lins?*" His voice bounces off the walls of the tiny apartment. He grips his handgun at his waist and lightly taps it against his sweatpants. "Yeah, I didn't think so," he mumbles low under his breath, but still loud enough for everyone to hear him. "Babygirl, come back here for a second and let me have a talk with you."

Hesitantly, Eva lets go of Kira's hand and walks to the back bedroom alone. As soon as Eva reaches the bedroom, Nox follows silently behind her. He closes the door, locking it from the other side. A poster of a human skull with a black snake crawling through its eye is tacked up on the outside of the door.

"We've gotta get outta here," I say through my teeth, as soon as I hear muffled voices talking in the other room. "That dude's whacked in the head!"

"Yeah, we'll find another way into Processing," Ria says in agreement. "Dealing with this lunatic isn't worth it."

"You can't just leave us here!" Kira shrieks a little too loud. Her eyes break away from the closed bedroom door for the first time.

All three of us turn to Rollins, waiting for him to answer.

"We're not going anywhere," my brother says deeply. "We came here to get Receivers and Kingston, and that's what we're gonna do." His eyes wander around the living room. A large, open cardboard box sits on the floor by the couch. It's filled with something dark.

Rollins walks over to the box, glancing up only once to check the closed bedroom door on the short trip across the living room. He reaches in and pulls out a Receiver. The corner of his mouth curls up as he shoves the device into his pocket.

In the bedroom, something made of glass smashes up against the wall, followed by a muffled, yet shrill screech by Eva.

"We gotta get out of here." My eyes fire back and forth between the bedroom door and my brother who is busy stuffing three more Receivers into his pockets.

"Sorry Kira," Rollins says as he reaches into the box to grab one more Receiver. "We've gotta run."

The bedroom door flies open and Nox spots my brother holding the Receiver, standing wide-eyed in the middle of his living room floor.

"Whatcha got there, *Raw-lins*?" Nox practically bounces out of the room with a smile on his face and steps toward my brother. There's no sign of Eva.

"We're gonna pay you for them," Rollins says with a slight stutter in his voice.

"Yeah, you keep talking about money," Nox begins, "but I don't see a Receiver there on your wrist, so how do you plan on paying me for them?"

My brother takes a small step away from the couch and lifts his hands in the air.

Nox raises his gun and points it at Rollins. He glances at us, still standing in the doorway. "Why don't you three join your friend, *Raw-lins* over here. He looks lonely."

As soon as he looks at my brother, I extend my hand, sending Nox flying back toward the wall on the opposite end of the apartment. His finger squeezes the trigger, midair, firing off a couple of shots before his head makes contact with the living room wall. Nox's unconscious body slumps down; his head lolls to the side. A small dent is left in the wall a couple of feet above where his body lays.

Rollins kicks the handgun out of Nox's hand and slides it over to me. I pick it up and stick it in the back waistline of my pants with only the handle showing.

"Good looking out, Nic," Rollins says. He keeps his eyes on the lifeless lowlife sprawled out before him. "Let's get moving. We got what we came for."

A shadow emerges from the bedroom doorway. Eva walks out, dazed.

"You okay, Eva?" Kira questions, as she studies her friend. Eva's face looks like it has grown at least two shades paler since entering the bedroom minutes earlier.

"Yeah," she says passively, holding a hand to the side of her head above her right eye. "Head hurts is all." Her eyes scan the room and land on Nox. Her pupils grow larger, slowly putting everything together.

Kira puts her arm around her friend's shoulders. "What happened in there?"

Eva ignores the questions and takes a few steps forward. She glares down at Nox, before firing a foot into the side of his ribs. The kick sends his unconscious body over an inch or two.

Kira hesitantly inches up behind Eva and begins to rub her back. "Let's get outta here before he wakes up." She sounds like she's trying to convince a toddler to do something they don't want to do.

Kira glances back at Rollins, then to me and Ria. "Thanks for that. I don't know what we would have done."

"Let's just say we're even now," Rollins says. "You promised us Receivers, and you came through." Rollins stuffs the final device down into his pocket, making both sides of his pants bulge out.

Once the three of us get outside of the apartment, I turn toward Rollins.

"How *were* you planning on paying for them?"

He eyes me. "No clue. I figured we'd come up with something, and we did."

CHAPTER 7

PROCESSING

We don't turn on any of the Receivers until we're outside of Processing.

"Mine's an old white guy," Ria says. She stares down at the device strapped to her wrist.

"Mine too." Rollins exhales in disgust. He swaps out his Receiver for the extra one in his pocket.

"This one's an old lady," I say, as soon as the profile of the previous owner's picture pops up on the screen. I take a bite from a Nutribar that Rollins just handed out to us.

"I have a fifteen year old boy on my extra." My brother flips the screen around to us for a look.

"Kind of looks like you, Nic" Ria says. She smiles, taking the device from Rollins and holds it up to my face. "Not as cute though."

"It's as close of a match as we're gonna get," my brother says. "Looks like you're going in alone, baby bro...or should I call you," he leans in closer to read the previous owner's name, "Jagger Jett?"

The speed of my heartbeat increases. I take the Receiver from Ria and strap it around my wrist. I click on the profile button and quickly review Jagger Jett's bio. Seems like a normal kid. I wonder how Nox got his Receiver.

"Here," Rollins says, as he grabs the active device around my wrist. "I'll input the ID number from my extra Receiver into yours. If you get into any trouble, hit the call button and let it connect. We'll be able to track you."

I exhale and glance over at Rollins before turning toward Ria. She gives me a hug and whispers in my ear, "Be careful."

I nod my head and I turn toward the door. "Let's do this."

* * *

As I swing the door open, a powerful odor wafts out that almost knocks me to the ground.   A crowd of people, many of them speaking different languages, fills the small waiting room.

"Citizen, your Receiver?" a robotic voice orders, as soon as the door closes behind me. A FootSoldier blocks the entrance, waiting to scan me.

I push up my sleeve and hold out the device in front of me. My hand trembles as I wait on the FootSoldier.

After a couple of seconds, the scan is over. "Take a seat. Your name will be called soon, Jag-ger Jett." The drone stumbles over my name, making it sound more like an alias than my real name.

My eyes sweep over the room.   The bright white painted walls immediately scream back at me, bringing me back to my old room at the Compound. The walls slope inward, which makes the room feel much smaller than it really is. All of the chairs are

35

occupied forcing the majority of the crowd to stand in the center. To my left, a large wooden desk is elevated on a platform, enclosed by a piece of bullet-proof glass that divides the room in half. A handful of clerks sit behind the desk, all of them typing away at the computers before them.

I take a few more steps forward before turning around to watch the FootSoldier scan a man who entered behind me. To the left of the desk, a door opens. The clerk allows a family of three through the door and down the sealed off hallway. That must be where they're holding Kingston.

The door clicks shut after the family shuffles inside the hallway. I glance back up at the clerks. The one who buzzed the family back is not paying attention to anyone but the crowd in front of him.

I inch a little closer toward the door, distancing myself from the rest of the waiting people. The next time the door opens, I'm getting in.

I study the clerk talking to a family with olive-colored skin on my side of the glass. The clerk's hand rests to the side. His fingers caress the tip of the button that releases the hold on the door. After a moment, his index finger straightens out and presses in the button. A loud buzzing sound follows, signaling the door is unlocked.

I take a small step toward the buzzing door, only to feel a heavy hand come down on my shoulder from behind. "Take a seat, Citizen. Move away from the door or you will be asked to leave. We are over occupancy at this time."

I nod my head toward the drone as it turns away from me. Beads of sweat trickle down my face. The buzzing sound from the door seems to be getting louder, it's the only thing I can hear now.

As soon as I see the FootSoldier is focused on someone else standing nearby, I dart toward the opening and push myself around the family, weaving myself in with them as if I belong. I keep my hand over the side of my face, careful to conceal it as we walk past a camera. Before I know it, we're all inside the hallway on the other side of the door.

The father flashes me a stern look warning me to back away from what I'm assuming is his teenage daughter. I heed the warning and fall a few steps back.

The olive skinned family enters the first room on the left, a holding area for the prisoner they are here to see. I peek into the room as I pass by. A table is setup in the center, with four chairs pushed in on all sides.

I quickly move deeper into the building.

Most of the doors are closed, but they all contain a small window, so I'm able to spy into each one.

So far I've come across maybe a dozen occupied rooms, but no Kingston.

Just as I'm starting to think that I might be in the wrong part of the building, I walk up to the final room in the hall. The only other door I haven't checked is windowless, appearing to lead into another hallway. I glance into the small window in front of me. My eyes find a group of a dozen prisoners all kneeling down on the floor. They're shackled to a steel bar running down the center of the room dividing the small holding area in half. Six prisoners kneel on one side of the bar, while the other six are on the other. All of them are males and not a single one of them is wearing a Receiver.

The lone prisoner with a shaved head lifts his face. His deadpan eyes gaze in front of him hopelessly like all the energy has been drained from his body. He readjusts his legs underneath him, probably in an attempt to get more comfortable.

Today's your lucky day, Kingston. I'm here to rescue you. Now my only problem is—how am I gonna get through this locked door and get you out of those cuffs without a key?

CHAPTER 8

UNDONE

The only open door in the hall is the one the olive skinned family entered earlier. I peer around the corner and spot a middle-aged Government employee in a shirt and tie exiting a room a few doors down. His attention is consumed entirely by a tablet in his hands. He holds a steaming cup of coffee in his mouth, the top edge of the Styrofoam cup wedged in-between his front teeth.

My eyes fall to the plastic keycard that hangs noticeably loose from a clip on his belt.

I reach my palm out and aim it at the man's waist. With a little careful effort, the metal clip holding the card to his belt snaps off.

Instinctively, as if he could sense the sudden pressure change on his belt, the man turns his head in my direction. I release my hold on the thin piece of plastic and drop my hand to my side. I casually turn my head and glance innocently down the opposite side of the hall, pretending to be patiently waiting on someone.

Out of the corner of my eye, I watch the man enter the room. He blindly reaches back to close the door with his only free hand.

I find the little plastic card lying on the carpet where the door meets its frame. Just as the door closes, I shoot my hand out and rocket the keycard the short distance down the hall and into my grasp.

I study the identification in my hand and note a smiling picture of the same Government employee staring up at me. "Dallard Winston," I read his name out loud. "Thank you for your service." The corner of my mouth curls up for a split second. Rollins would have been proud of me back there.

The main door leading out to the lobby buzzes opens. Uh-oh. I freeze, not knowing what to do. I back up against the closed door behind me as several voices draw closer. My free hand reaches back and grabs onto the thin, steel door handle. I pull down on it, but it's locked. I already knew that.

I take my eyes off the hallway for a second, long enough to swipe the card on the key reader to the right of the door. A green light blinks three times and releases the lock on the door. I stumble inside, just as the group of employees turns the corner. I watch as they pass and enter another door at the end of the hall.

As soon as the voices are gone, I poke my head out. The coast is clear.

Time to get Kingston and get out of this place.

I step back out into the hallway. The temperature seems to have risen a few degrees in the twenty seconds I was hiding in the room. Beads of sweat run down my forehead as I head in the direction of the holding room.

I peer into the window and spot Kingston staring miserably down at the floor. I rapidly swipe the keycard through the reader. The green light flashes and the door clicks to allow me in.

As soon as I step inside, all of the prisoners turn to glance up at me. From the expressions on their faces, I can tell they were expecting someone else. Kingston's eyes grow large.

"What took you so long, mate?" Kingston flashes me a smile. Everyone else in the room stares back at me with confused expressions.

"Yeah, what took you so long?" a fat teen mockingly shouts, kneeling down next to Kingston.

A chorus of "yeahs" fills the room.

I study the bar and the steel cuffs Kingston has shackled around his wrists. The keycard won't unlock the cuffs. I didn't think this through. Out of the corner of my eye, I spot a security camera flashing a red bulb at me. I *really* didn't think this one through.

I turn back toward the door, and for a split second, I consider making a break for it. I can regroup with Rollins and Ria outside. We'll figure something else out…a new plan. But there's no time.

I focus back on the steel bar again. It seems to be attached to the floor on both ends by a few small screws.

I extend my hand and begin to rapidly unscrew each screw, each one flying up in the air like a miniature tornado, before bouncing worthlessly off to the side. The prisoners begin to yank on the bar before all of the screws are removed. With one final pull, they forcefully rip the bar clean out of the floor. With their hands still cuffed, they make a mad dash for the only exit.

I grab Kinston, pulling him up from the floor and out of the room. While the group of eleven prisoners heads down the hallway toward the lobby and the buzzing door, Kingston and I duck off in the opposite direction. There has to be another way out.

I pull the keycard from my pocket and scan it on the reader for the door at the end of the hall. The door opens into another hallway identical to the one we were just in.

41

"Can't thank you enough, Nic. I really thought that was it for me."

Kingston uses the side of his sleeve to wipe sweat off his forehead. His hands remain shackled together.

"Hey don't thank me yet." My eyes nervously search down the new hall we just entered. "Wait until we find a way outta this place, then you can thank me. Besides, no one gets left behind, right?"

CHAPTER 9

LOCATION

I find an exit sign about midway down the long, barren hallway before us. I tap Kingston on the side of his arm. "Come on."

As we make a break for the exit, the door on the opposite end of the hall opens. Multiple drones step into the hallway, each armed with a large weapon. The lead drone's eyes flash down the corridor and begin a scan on my Receiver.

"Halt, Jag-gar Jett! You are wanted for trespassing on Government property."

I don't stop. Without turning around, I know Kingston is right behind me.

The lead drone aims its gun in our direction.

"This is your last warning, Jag-gar Jett!"

I dive for the keycard reader and pull the door open, all in one motion, swinging it toward the drones. Bright sunlight floods through the opening, as bullets spray across the front side of the steel door that is now a barrier and our only protection from the drones' deadly weapons.

I pull Kingston toward me, using the chain shackling his wrists together. Together we fall outside in a tangled heap and fumble to pull the door closed behind us.

We find ourselves in an empty, narrow alleyway, only large enough for us to stand shoulder to shoulder next to each other. The neighboring building's outside shiny steel wall is the same as the outside of Processing—it must be another Government building.

Jumping up, I pull Kingston to his feet and the two of us run wildly down the alleyway that leads us to the street in front of Processing. At least two dozen FootSoldier drones are scattered all around, questioning the large mass of people who have gathered in front of the building. Citizens are handcuffed and sitting down away from the crowd in circled groups.

"I think we need to find another route, mate. They got this one covered."

The group in front of the building has grown since I originally entered. I quickly scan the crowd looking for Rollins and Ria but come up empty. I shake my head and spot Kingston staring at me out of the corner of my eye, as if he's waiting on me to make a move. Am I leading things now?

"Rollins and Ria were supposed to meet us out front." My eyes do one more quick sweep across the mob of people. A group of older men yell at a FootSoldier scanning their Receivers as the drone violently shoves another person up against the wall. "But I don't see them anywhere."

"We can't stay here, Nic." Kingston's eyes flash back toward the door we just exited. "Looks like it's about to get a little more crowded."

I glance back at the door just as the tip of an automatic gun carefully inches out.

With no other choice, we put our heads down and melt into the crowd. We push and shove our way through the people, trying to stay as far away from the drones as possible. Kingston stays right behind me, close enough that he steps on the heels of my boots twice. He keeps his hands hidden under the front of his shirt to conceal his cuffs.

"Let's try to move over there," I say, nodding to the left as I turn back to Kingston. A man to my right shoves past me, knocking me off my feet. After tumbling to the ground, I look to find a FootSoldier standing over me.

"Receiver, Citizen."

My eyes flash over to Kingston. He stands frozen with a bewildered expression. So this is where it's going to end for me? In the middle of the street in Srune?

A gun goes off in the crowd. The entire mob shifts to the side as people try to flee. A group of teens jump over me and strike the FootSoldier, providing the distraction I need to escape. I hop back up and duck my head down. The torrent of people carries me away from the drone and the center of the mob.

I turn around to search for Kingston.

He's gone.

Even if I wanted to go back to look for him, I would never be able to get through the aggressive crowd. I suddenly feel like a fish trying to swim upstream.

Something Rollins told me earlier pops in my head. In all of the commotion, I forgot our Receivers are linked. I glance down at my wrist where Jagger Jett's Receiver is still activated. I press the call button, holding it in for a second before releasing it. In no time Rollins and Ria will know exactly where I am, and then we can find

Kingston together. He's gotta be around here somewhere. I drop my wrist to my side, feeling a little bit more confident. A smile builds across my face.

Then it hits me.

I jerk to a stop.

By sending my location to Ria and Rollins, I've also just alerted the Government and the drones searching for me of my exact coordinates.

CHAPTER 10

JUST BREATHE

I move as quickly as I can away from the crowd and cut down another alley a few streets over. I scramble behind a dumpster that reeks of urine and rotten food and plop down on the ground to catch my breath.

Something sharp pokes me in the pocket.

I reach my hand in and pull out the flash drive. I completely forgot I still had it.

I pop the small drive into the side of the Receiver. While the file loads, I crane my head around the side of the dumpster to make sure I'm still alone. From where I sit, I can see all the way to the street. People continue to pass by, moving away from the Processing building, but none enter the alleyway.

I rest my head against the side of the dumpster. A 3D image of the words *Project Transporter* fades in, hovering an inch or two in the air above the device strapped around my wrist.

A video begins, time-stamped in the corner with a date from a few years ago. An image of a Healer comes into focus, along with a single man dressed in a white lab coat over his clothes. His face is partially hidden with a mask, covering his mouth and nose. The man's eyes shift back and forth, almost as if he's waiting on something to happen, before he turns toward the coffin-like rectangular box and lifts its hood. The 3D image slightly shakes as the camera operator moves in closer to get an inside shot of the Healer. That's when I notice it's not a Healer. It's similar to the medical device, probably made using the same shell, but the input screen looks different. Another person enters the picture and slowly steps up to the device, then lies down inside. I peek my head around the edge of the dumpster again.

Still nothing.

I continue watching the video and inch closer to the image. The man is lying in the device completely still, his arms crossed over his chest as if he's hugging himself. His eyes are closed. He wears a black padded vest with a single yellow lightning bolt on it over his white T-shirt.

Why would that doctor risk his life to get us this video? There has to be more to it.

"Hey! You seen that kid everyone's looking for?" I hear a voice shout at the opposite end of the alleyway.

I jump, subconsciously turning my Receiver down toward the dumpster. I stick my head out and find a homeless-looking man walking by the mouth of the alleyway.

"He's long gone, if he knows what's good for him." The owner of the voice continues up the road, yelling at someone ahead of him.

I focus back on the silent video playing. The man in the white lab coat closes the lid over the person in the vest and begins to type in a series of code into the keypad on the side of the machine.

Then he steps out of the picture. A massive neon blue light erupts underneath the lid, squeezing out sheets of aqua. The 3D image of the video is as blue as a cloudless sky on a spring day.

Suddenly the blue light recedes into nothing. The man in the white lab coat comes back into view and lifts the lid to the device to reveal the man in the vest has vanished.

The 3D image of the Healer…or whatever that thing is disappears.

The screen goes black for a second and words begin to fill the screen.

Your mission is to locate a Transporter. Go back in time and end the Tele program before it has the chance to begin. You must find the source.

Go back in time *and* end the Tele program? That's it? I might as well save the entire planet while I'm at it. I shake my head in disgust. I just want my family back, not to play hero.

"The fugitive is close." I hear a robotic-sounding voice echo behind me. "His beacon is going off at this location."

I steal a quick look around the edge of the dumpster. Three armed FootSoldiers enter the alley from the street. Their red eyes carefully scan their surroundings, sweeping back and forth across the alley as they slowly get closer to where I hide.

About twenty feet away, I watch a small black and white striped kitten jump out of an overflowing trashcan. The lead drone stops and lifts his gun all in one motion. Before the cat's paws even hit the cement, the FootSoldier fires at the furry animal, incinerating it into a puff of smoke and ash.

The three drones move closer to the garbage can to inspect its remains. The drone who took the shot scans the fresh stain on the concrete with its mechanical eyes. All of its attention is now on the dead cat.

I take in a big gulp of air, attempting to swallow down the hard lump stuck in the back of my throat. I steal one more look around the edge of the dumpster, before stealthy hopping over the side and falling somewhat gracefully into the mostly-filled trash container. The stench of urine is immediately intensified as I close the lid over me.

"This way," one drone orders the other two. "He is here somewhere."

I hear the FootSoldiers' heavy footsteps move closer. The drones do not even try to conceal their location. Machines show no fear.

I burrow myself farther down in the dumpster and cover myself the best I can in the darkness with who knows what people have thrown out.

The lid flies open over me. My face is covered, but I can sense the drones moving trash around, searching for me.

A warm liquid drips down onto my face. Some of it even trickles into my mouth and nose as I attempt to breathe. It tastes like something sour that went bad weeks ago.

More light finds my face as they get closer. One of the drones picks up a box that's covering one of my feet. I can feel the warm sunlight beam down on the tip of my shoe. This is it.

I've gotta make a run for it.

My breathing becomes noticeably heavier and more rapid, trying to psyche myself up. It's now or never.

Just as I'm starting to push myself up, I hear one of the drones call into whoever is controlling them.

"He's not here, Commander," the robotic-monotone voice says inches over me. "The beacon must have picked up another source."

The lid to the dumpster closes and I'm enveloped in darkness once again.

That was too close.

After allowing enough time for the FootSoldiers to exit the alleyway, I peak my head out to make sure I'm alone. I hop out of the dumpster, wondering why the Government was able to track me, but not Rollins or Ria. I glance down at the screen on my Receiver and read the words, not believing what I'm seeing.

In order to succeed in your mission, you must take out the creator of the Tele program, Josiah McCready. This is the only way.

The flash drive, still connected the side of the Receiver, begins to emit a trail of gray smoke as it begins to self-destruct.

Dad is the creator of the Tele program?

CHAPTER 11

LOST AND FOUND

If that doctor thinks I'm gonna kill my own father, he's crazy!

I rip the Receiver off my wrist and toss it into the dumpster. There's no sense in letting the Government know where I'm headed.

Where *am* I headed?

In a daze, I make my way toward the entrance of the alley. I'm all alone. No Rollins, no Ria, no Kingston—plus my parents are missing. Maybe giving myself up wouldn't be the end of the world?

My eyes focus on the ground in front of me. I feel lost.

"Don't you know it's not safe for fugitives to be walking around in the streets by themselves?" a deep voice calls out to me from around the corner. "If the wrong person finds them…"

Rollins and Ria jump out from around the corner with matching grins.

"Nic!" Ria shrieks, pushing my brother out of the way. She runs up and gives me a giant hug.

"You just missed three Soldiers," I announce boastfully, holding Ria close to me. "I took care of them though. Didn't think you'd show." I pull back, but still hold her waist tightly.

"Always, baby bro. You can count on that." Rollins walks up and pats me on the top of the head.

"Guess you didn't have any luck with Kingston?" Ria asks, her face slightly scrunched up. She takes a small step back, assumingly to escape my rancid odor.

"No, we got out, but then I lost him in the crowd out in front of Processing." I look around the street, and then back to Ria and my brother. "I have no clue what was going on out there. It was pure chaos—too many people and too many drones. We just got separated. The FootSoldiers tracked me down here."

Rollins glances down at my wrist. "Good job ditching the dirty Receiver. Too bad the FootSoldiers beat us here though." Rollins takes the extra Receiver out of his pocket and hands it to me. "Put this on. If anything, you won't stick out for not having one."

"Just don't let anyone scan you," Ria adds. She shows me the Receiver she wears around her wrist is not powered on.

I nod my head.

"You still have that file the doctor gave us at the station?"

The file.

"They want us to kill Dad," I blurt out. I shamefully look away from both Rollins and Ria. "I plugged in the flash drive and it talked about going back in time to kill Dad—the creator of the Tele program."

My brother stares at me blankly. His mouth hangs slightly agape, not knowing what to say or do.

"Dad wasn't a scientist though. They must have him confused with someone else!" I scream at Rollins.

"When I was young, I remember going to a lab with Dad a few times," Rollins says slowly, as if trying to remember. "It was right after you were born. Mom couldn't watch me for some reason, so Dad took me to work with him."

Multiple gunshots erupt down the street sending a mob of people rushing off in the opposite direction of Processing.

Following the crowd, a pair of FootSoldiers comes into view. One turns toward us and its eyes scan the alley.

Right away a loud buzzing sound fills the sky.

"We've gotta go to Silo," Rollins says as he looks up. "Maybe we can find Dad's old lab and—,"

"Hawk!" I shout out as I reach for Ria's hand.

We take off running, racing down the alleyway in the only direction possible—away from the street. We pass the dumpster, and about fifty feet down, we run into a wall.

We're trapped.

I bend over, hands on knees, as I try to catch my breath. I glance up at Rollins. His eyes scale the top of the chain-link fence. The building behind the fence is multi-floored, but just where the fence ends, there's a busted out window we can duck into.

"You two ready?"

I straighten up and nod. Rollins lifts his hand and vaults Ria and then me up and over the fence, and through the open window of the abandoned building. It's completely dark inside. The power's off, but it's more than that. The walls and floor—everything around us is draped in black. Either a fire took this place out, or someone overdid it with the black paint.

Rollins joins us through the window.

"Come on, let's go!" he shouts, not waiting to see if we follow him.

Gunfire explodes outside, spraying the backside of the building with bullets.

We sprint across the room just as something small flies in through the open window and clanks down on the floor.

"Take cover!" Rollins shouts. He dives, shoving Ria and I toward the stairwell. An explosion goes off in the room that takes out the majority of the floor we just stood on.

We fly down the stairs, all the way down to the bottom level. The first floor is identical to the fourth—dark.

I duck my head outside the door. No aerial drones. No FootSoldiers. The street seems quiet as we cautiously leave the building.

"We've gotta make it ten blocks over to the downtown station. It's pretty much a straight shot." Rollins glances toward the street.

From a distance, I spot a giant screen hanging down from one of the skyscrapers downtown, similar to The Beacon back home in Sol. A photo of me is plastered across the front of the enormous video screen with the words FUGITIVE WANTED in all capital letters at the bottom.

"Look," I say, as I point a shaky finger in the direction of the Jumbotron.

Ria stares at the sign. "We may wanna rethink our route to the station."

CHAPTER 12

MFC

Cars are randomly parked on both sides of the street outside of the building. Most of them seem to have been abandoned, covered in dust.

Rollins walks over to an already busted out window of an old convenience store that looks like it went out of business years ago. He pulls a cinder block out of the broken glass and debris. Holding it with a single hand, he lets the brick hang to his side as he glances down the street. He walks up to the closest car and tosses the cinder block at the driver's side window. The glass shatters upon impact.

My brother yanks open the door. Little pieces of glass blanket the two front seats. Rollins pulls a knife out of his back pocket and, with a flick of the wrist, a blade emerges. He climbs into the driver's seat and pops off the center of the steering wheel, uncovering a small, dark screen. Several multi-colored, loose wires dangle below. He cuts two of the wires that feed into the screen and twists them together.

I look over at Ria. She's carefully watching my brother, probably wondering where he learned how to do all of this. I'm wondering the same thing.

Rollins presses his face up to the little screen inside of the steering wheel and alters the system's configurations, tricking the vehicle into thinking he's the owner. The engine sputters to life. The small car jerks back about an inch, and then forward a couple of inches.

"Climb in," Rollins says, as he snaps the casing back over the screen. "We've gotta make that next MagneTrain if we want any chance at escaping this place."

As soon as Ria and I hop into the back seat of the tiny car, Rollins takes off. We pull out onto the main street and all I can focus on is the enormous Jumbotron with my wanted photo on it filling the sky.

"They could have at least used a cuter picture of you," Ria says in an attempt to break the awkward silence in the car.

No one says a word. I hear Rollins deeply exhale. His eyes find the rearview mirror for a second before moving back to the road. The photo on display is from a security feed back in Sol or maybe it's from the MagneTrain station in Srune. I'm wearing the same clothes that I have on now, so there's no telling.

"We have company," Rollins says as he adjusts the mirror to a better angle.

Ria and I both turn around to find a Government military police vehicle gaining speed behind us.

"That MP's been tailing us since we got onto this street. I probably should have taken some back roads, but I didn't think we'd have any trouble until we got to the station." My brother's eyes anxiously flash back and forth from the mirror to the road in front of him.

The military police vehicle turns on its overhead emergency red lights, ordering Rollins to stop. Instead, my brother steps on the gas.

"We all know what's going to happen if I pull over." Rollins's eyes only concentrate on the road before us now. "Hang on!"

As we take the next right, the right half of the car slightly lifts itself off the ground by an inch or two, holding its balance long enough to go around the corner. We cut down the narrow side street and make an immediate left, an equally narrow street only big enough for one car to pass at a time. Apartment buildings line either side of the road, close enough to the street that we are able to see right inside the units. Most of the rooms on the bottom floor are vacant only every third unit or so is occupied.

My eyes drift ahead, halfway feeling shame for invading people's privacy, but more for seeing how bad their living conditions are. Things are bad in Sol, but it's nothing like this.

Up ahead I spot a white sheet with something written across it flapping in the wind. The top half is nailed against the side of the building and hangs down over the bottom floor's windows.

"Stay away," I mumble out loud, but quiet enough that no one can hear. I shake my head and steal a glance back at the MP vehicle still viciously chasing us.

An idea comes to mind.

As we reach the end of the building, I extend my arm out the window and use my telekinesis to rip the sheet free from its hold. I fling my wrist and toss the large, hole-filled cloth behind us like a rag, confident it will land exactly where I want it to—across the MP's windshield.

Rollins sharply takes the next corner and leads us onto another narrow street. I watch as the military police vehicle attempts to follow us, but instead ends up skidding into the side of the rundown apartment building, crashing into the bottom floor. A family runs out through the opening yelling something at the confused officers who remain seated in the vehicle. Both airbags deploy about ten seconds too late.

"We lost them!" I yell with excitement. Ria and Rollins both raise a closed fist in the air to celebrate, leaving the MPs behind us.

"That was too close." Ria stares forward at my brother.

He turns his attention to the rearview mirror.

Boom!

Another MP vehicle materializes out of nowhere, racing up from behind to ram us. Rollins grips the wheel as our small car pulls to the left and right, slightly out of control.

Ria reaches out for my hand but her eyes remain glued to the front windshield. I squeeze her hand and pull her closer to me.

"Wish we would've picked something with a little more juice," Rollins mumbles to himself as he grits his teeth. He slams on the brakes and takes the next right, and then the following left, getting us back onto the main road in the direction of the station. The MP vehicle mirrors our every move, refusing to let us escape.

Rollins swerves onto the left side of the road—toward oncoming traffic, weaving us in and out of the cars racing toward us.

The Jumbotron with my wanted picture on it comes back into view. Just below the screen, I read and shout the words, "MagneTrain Northeast Station!"

"I'm gonna pull up and you two jump out." Rollins keeps both hands firmly on the wheel. He glares back at us in the mirror. "I'll meet you on the train." A siren continues to wail behind us, alerting everyone in the vicinity of the high speed chase.

"No!" I scream out, matching Rollins's glare in the rear mirror. "We stay together!"

"Just do it!" He breaks his stare to concentrate back on the road.

A shot goes off and hits the back window above my head.

"They're shooting at us!" Ria yells out.

Three more bullets pierce the window, shattering what's left of the glass all over the backseat and us.

Ria screams again as my brother slams on the brakes and yanks the wheel hard to the right. He pulls out into the middle of the road and veers across three lanes of traffic, forcing moving vehicles to swerve out of the way. A car driving in the correct direction swerves to miss us, but slams into the front end of the driver's side of our vehicle. The backside of our car fishtails across the farthest lane. I close my eyes and lean my head back on the headrest until the car finally stops spinning. Glass from the windshield explodes upon impact as we strike the side of an already parked car.

Silence.

"Is anyone hurt?" I hear Rollins call out from the front seat. At the sound of his voice I open my eyes. "Nic? You're okay!" He begins stroking my hair, sporting a huge grin across his face.

"I'm okay, I'm okay," I say, as I pull away from him and turn toward Ria. She's awake, but mute, and looking like she just saw a ghost. "Ria, are you okay?"

She nods her head once, her distant gaze not finding mine.

Rollins reaches over and kicks open the passenger side door on the far side of the car. It flips open, almost tearing in half like a piece of construction paper. Both driver's side doors are caved in, pushed up against the parked car we smashed into. Rollins pries open the back passenger side door from the outside and pulls us both out. As soon as we're free, we run. I look up and I'm met again with the enormous wanted picture of myself that hangs off the side of a downtown skyscraper in Srune, and we're headed straight for it.

CHAPTER 13

DOWN

I glance back at the smashed up car behind us, mangled on the side of the road with both passenger side doors left ajar. A trail of smoke escapes from the hood. There's already a crowd of people gathered around the car that struck us—the vehicle remains in the far right lane of the busy road. A confused owner is just now exiting the car.

"Hope everyone's okay." Ria steals a glance back at the chaotic scene building behind us. She looks toward me and waits for a response. All I can manage is a single nod as we approach our destination.

We enter through the station's main doors and race through the lobby, darting around both incoming and exiting passengers. I spot a train sitting on the magnet tracks with its doors open.

An unexpected loud siren goes off that echoes off the walls and marble flooring under our feet.

"There has been a breach in security," an electronic-monotone voice announces over the loudspeakers that fills the lobby of the station. "We ask all passengers to report to their final destination. The next MagneTrain will be leaving before the scheduled departure time."

They're trying to trap us here!" Rollins shouts through his teeth. He turns back toward me and Ria. "We've gotta get on that train."

In a single leap, Rollins jumps the turnstiles' barrier that divides the lobby in half. Ria and I follow closely behind.

"Hey! Those kids didn't pay!" An older woman points us out in the crowd on the opposite side of the turnstile. A few eyes find us, but no one does anything. Normally a passenger would hold their Receiver up to the device to dock money for their train ride—two things we do not have.

Rollins darts onto the boarding platform just as the train's doors close right in his face. He bangs a closed fist on the tinted window. Ria and I run up behind him out of breath. We're too late. There's a child on the other side of the window looking out, maybe five or six years old, loosely holding onto his mother's hand. The woman looks down at her Receiver, her lips moving as she reads something off the screen. The boy stares back at us with a blank expression.

The MagneTrain shifts forward, taking the train car with the little boy and his mother away.

"Come on," Rollins says. He starts off in the direction of the back end of the train. "We need to find another way on."

I spot a pair of FootSoldiers forcing passengers to move behind the yellow painted line that divides the platform in half. Because of the speed the MagneTrain can reach, no one is allowed over the yellow line once a train is moving or they may get sucked under the tracks.

I make eye contact with one of the drones. It freezes and radios in to its controller.

We duck behind a cement column on the opposite side of the yellow line. I look over the edge of the platform as the MagneTrain picks up speed. There's at least a ten or fifteen foot drop down to the tracks.

"Looks like the end of the train is coming," Rollins says. His eyes search down the dark tunnel behind the train. "We're gonna have to jump on as it passes. There's an emergency hatch on the back of all of these MagneCars."

I steal a glance around the large post that extends up into the ceiling. The two drones have abandoned their crowd control and are making their way through the crowd in our direction.

"Rollins?" I say, as I duck back around the post. "I think we've been found."

Rollins quickly looks over before inching a little closer to the edge of the platform.

"Freeze, Citizen!" One of the FootSoldiers has spotted Rollins. It grips a gun firmly across its armored chest. Both machines plant their feet firmly on the cement floor.

The crowd of people waiting for the next train obediently stay behind the yellow line, but they watch us intently, anticipating a climactic end to the scene unfolding.

"Just concentrate on making that last car," Rollins says. The pair of FootSoldiers stay firm and hold their ground. "I'm gonna cause a distraction."

Rollins walks out from around the large post with both hands raised over his head. "Don't shoot! Don't shoot!" he yells. "I'm unarmed!"

I look over toward the people behind the yellow line again. There seems to be some kind of commotion going on; the crowd unexpectedly parts down the middle as someone pushes through, yelling at the top of their lungs.

Kingston emerges from the mass of people with a raised palm outstretched above his head. His ponytail sways back and forth, matching his movements as he runs straight for the first drone in his path. He hits the machine in the torso with his telekinesis, careening it to the opposite end of the station. It strikes a wall and crumbles to the floor, unable to pick itself back up.

The second drone turns around and raises its gun. Kingston aims his hand and rockets it back toward the tracks. The FootSoldier smashes against the side of the moving MagneTrain as it continues to build speed. Its head becomes wedged between two MagneCars, dragging the drone down into the tunnel until it disappears into the darkness.

"The last car is coming!" Ria yells as she keeps her eyes on the end of the train. She grabs my hand and we jump together, landing easily on the rear small platform of the final train car.

"Where's Rollins?" I shout. My eyes search the station's loading area. "He was just here!"

Kingston doesn't break his running stride. Just as he reaches the edge of the loading area, he leaps into the air, his legs kick out below him looking for level ground. The front of his boot hits the edge of the car's rear platform, causing him to land in an awkward roll next to us.

Ria helps Kingston to his feet, while I continue to search the Srune station's platform as it whizzes by. Maybe another drone got him?

"There he is!" Ria shouts as she points my brother out in the crowd.

Rollins comes into view and I notice he has stolen one of the drone's guns. He sprints across the station's loading area, quickly running out of room before the start of a tunnel. "He's never gonna make it," I mumble, even though I refuse to believe it myself.

"Come on, Rollins!" Ria shouts. Both of her hands grip the railing in front of her. "Just drop the gun!"

I reach my hand out, begging Rollins to jump for it.

Rollins runs faster and matches the train's speed. Just as he's about to run out of pavement, he leaps for the train and extends his arm out toward my hand, his fingers just barely touching mine. The gun falls from his grip and clanks down onto the tracks behind him. His other hand reaches for the railing on the back of the train car.

Kingston grabs my brother's hand that's now gripped around the railing as I reach for his loose one.

"Help me pull him in!" I shout with a struggle.

Ria sticks her hand out to help me and, as if in slow motion, I watch as Rollins falls backward into the darkness of the tracks. I reach for him, using my force to suspend him in the air for a second or two, before pulling him back up. Sometimes I forget all about my ability. Rollins lands on the car's little rear platform in a thump. My brother lies there for a few seconds with his eyes closed, catching his breath.

"Sure hope this one's heading to Silo," he says. A sudden smile erupts across his face as he continues to take in deep breaths.

With everything we've been through, all we could do is laugh.

CHAPTER 14

WAR PAINT

"If it wasn't for that stunt with the MP in front of the station, I wouldn't have found you," Kingston says. He follows Rollins inside the train car through the rear exit door. Ria and I follow and slide the door closed behind us.

Three benches sit unoccupied in the back of the MagneCar next to the exit. The four of us plop down onto the hard plastic seats, Ria and me on one seat and Rollins and Kingston on the seat facing us. Ria puts her hand on my knee and pulls me in a little closer, resting the side of her head on my shoulder.

"Why do I get the feeling everyone's staring at us?" she quietly asks.

I crane my head out into the aisle. Every pair of eyes in the train car is fixed on our back two benches. I look at Ria, and then over at my brother and Kingston. All of our clothes are torn and ripped, our faces marked with various cuts and gashes like war paint. We look like we just fought in hand-to-hand combat and lost.

"So, what did I miss?" Kingston questions my brother. Their bench faces the rear of the MagneCar so they cannot see any of the passengers filling the front.

As soon as Rollins begins to update Kingston about what was on the flash drive—our father's possible lab in Silo and how he's the creator of the Tele program—I tune out. I scan the inside of the cabin again. The other passengers have moved on from the initial shock of our tattered appearance and are now mindlessly staring down at the devices strapped around their wrists.

I smile to myself for a brief second until I catch the stare of a woman in the front of the train car. She has on blue scrubs, like nurses wear at the hospital. Tiny wrinkles outline the outer part of her eyes, making her look older than she probably is.

I slouch down in my seat. She glances quickly down to her Receiver before looking back in our direction again. She lightly taps the man sitting next to her on his arm. He leans toward her, but his eyes stay glued to the device around his own wrist.

She leans over toward the man, whispering something low as she pushes her Receiver in front of his face.

Noticeably perturbed, the man peers down at her screen. His eyes shift to the back of the train car, locating our bench. We make eye contact for a brief second before he looks back at the image on the woman's Receiver again.

The woman types something into her screen. Her eyes jump back and forth from the device to our bench.

I lean in toward the other group. "I think we've been recognized."

Rollins releases a deep groan as he twists his body around to steal a peek over the top of the bench's headrest. Kingston tenses up and pulls his shoulders back.

"The man and woman in the front?" Rollins questions. The couple awkwardly turns away from us after being spotted. "At least they're making it obvious."

"All passengers on the Sol MagneTrain," a dull electronic-sounding announcement begins over the car's speakers, "we will be arriving in Silo momentarily. Please make your Receiver available for scan before departure. Close out all other applications and remove any garments that may be covering the device. Thank you for choosing Sol's MagneTrain Services for all of your transportation needs, where your safety is our top priority."

I reach back and pull down on the handle of the exit door. It doesn't budge.

"Locked?" Ria asks, already knowing the answer.

I nod my head. "We're trapped." I expect Rollins to have a plan like usual. The expression on his face tells me he has nothing.

I swallow hard. We're sitting ducks here. My eyes move over to the window. The reflection of my dirty, pale face bounces off the glass, but beyond that all I see is flat, brown land extending out as far as I can see.

Then the scenery is gone.

The desolate landscape disappears and is replaced with black nothingness. We've entered another tunnel. This one must lead into the Silo station.

The inside of the train car goes dark, as only a few dim overhead lights flash on and off. I lean forward and rest my forehead in the palms of my hands. *Think!*

I concentrate on eight bolts in the floor that surrounds my feet. They form a square about the size of a small door, or possibly an emergency hatch for the cabin. I lean forward to Rollins and motion down to what could be a way out.

My brother nods. He turns to check on the couple in the front of the car again.

I hover both of my hands over the floor and begin to unscrew each of the bolts. Each bolt rotates so quickly they release a sharp whistling sound, loud enough to pull wandering passengers' eyes to the back two benches again.

Ria's hand falls off my knee, signaling me to stop. I'm halfway through the eight bolts, when I look up. The door in the front of the train car slides open; three FootSoldier drones stomp in, all three with raised guns.

"Nicholas McCready, you are wanted by the Sol Government for treason, trespassing..."

The drones continue with my list of charges as they make their way down the center aisle to the rear of the car. Everyone's eyes shift from the front door to the back of the train car. A few nearby passengers hold up their wrists, their Receivers recording the scene.

I lower my hands and get back to work. Without being told, Rollins, Kingston, and Ria each take a bolt and, soon the panel is free.

Kingston lifts the heel of his boot and slams it back down over the square piece of steel flooring. The cover to the hatch snaps free and gets sucked up under the train as a loud, howling roar fills the cabin.

"I'm going first," Kingston says. He's already inching his way into the hole. "To make sure it's safe." He hooks his legs around a metal bar and swings himself under the floorboard of the train. "See you all on the other side!" he shouts before disappearing.

"Ria, you're next," I say, as I keep my voice low, "and then Rollins. I'm the one they're after. I'll go last." I scratch my forehead and then the top of my head.

70

"And that's exactly why you and Ria are gonna go next," my brother says. He leans into me. "I'll follow you."

I glance back at the drones knowing there's no time for an argument. I help Ria to the floor.

"Freeze, Fugitive," the lead drone says, his red eyes focused on me. "You are wanted by the Sol Government for treason, trespassing, murder..." The drone redundantly continues with my list of charges, as if I didn't hear them all the first time.

I slowly stand and raise my hands over my head. My legs begin to shake. "Don't hurt them. It's me you're after."

Ria has already started crawling under the train's floorboard, only the top half of her face is visible now. She looks back. "Nic! No! What're you doing?"

Rollins springs up from behind the row of seats. At the same time, we both direct our palms at the pair of FootSoldiers standing before us. Their steel bodies fly into the closed door in the front of the train car. If anything, we bought ourselves an extra ten or fifteen seconds.

My brother and I dive for the hole. Rollins helps me in first before quickly following. I shimmy myself up the large pipe running down the middle of the train car. I can feel the pipe shake as the drones step heavily across the floorboards above me. I steal a quick look down into the darkness, remembering how deep the tracks seemed earlier at the Srune station.

Rollins inches up below me and shouts something I can't understand over the roaring wind.

"Let...Go!" he yells again.

This time I'm able to hear it. Wait, what? My eyes bug out, emphatically shaking my head.

"On three!" Rollins yells, ignoring me.

71

"One...! Two...! Three...!

I close my eyes, take a deep breath, and let the strong current rip me free. My body shoots backward to Rollins where he grabs me with one arm and pulls me in. I wrap my arms around his forearm and hook a leg around one of his legs.

He lets go of the pipe he's holding onto and shoots us both back together to the rear of the train, flying faster than I ever thought possible.

CHAPTER 15

RUNAWAY TRAIN

Rollins lies on top of me with his burly chest wedged up against my face, making it difficult to breathe. The hard track digs into my back. I slap at the sides of his forearms and finally succeed at pushing him off me as I grasp for air. The train has disappeared, along with the loud noise that filled the dark tunnel.

I sit up and peer around at our surroundings. I can't see two inches in front of my face. It's that dark.

"Think Ria and Kingston are around here somewhere?" I ask, turning in the direction of where I think Rollins is lying.

"There's no telling," my brother says. He uses my pants leg to pull himself up. "Depends when they let go. They could be anywhere." He grunts as he stands up, pulling me up by the arm next to him. "Either way, we need to get out of this tunnel. Who knows when the next train will show."

"I can't see anything." I turn around blindly, trying to find the outline of the tunnel behind us. "Unreal."

"Should we wait for another MagneTrain to come along and provide us with some light?" There's a strong layer of sarcasm in his voice. "That way you can see where you're going?"

"Yeah, that sounds like the most logical thing to do. Hopefully one will come chugging along any minute," I say with the same amount of attitude.

Rollins grabs me by the top of the head and ruffles up my hair, laughing. "Come on." He puts the crook of his arm around my neck and pulls me in closer.

For a second, a smile forms across my face. Then I remember what we were asked to do by the doctor—to take out Dad and the Tele program with him. My mouth tightens as I erase the happy expression from my face.

* * *

"Stop!"

My boot kicks the steel track in front of me. We've been walking for what feels like at least an hour and this is the first time either one of us has uttered a word.

"Do you feel that?" Rollins questions. I sense that he is squatting down by my feet.

I crouch to join him. He is gripping the side of the track. I place my hand almost on top of his.

I shake my head. "I don't feel—"

But then I do. Very faintly, I feel the steel between my fingers beginning to vibrate. Then it hits me—

"Is that what I think it is?"

"Yeah," Rollins says, standing back up, "but there's no telling how far away it is. It could even be in another tunnel. Just to be sure, let's move a little quicker."

Rollins grabs me by the arm and yanks me down the tracks. My boots keep tripping me up since I'm forced to take wider strides to keep up with him. He doesn't let me fall though, always keeping one hand wrapped around my upper arm. Both sides of the track are elevated slightly—maybe two or three feet high, which helps us to walk in a somewhat straight line.

"I think I see something up ahead," my brother says, between breaths. "A light."

We pick up the pace, shuffling our feet.

"It looks like a flashlight," I say. "Ria? Kingston?" I yell.

Rollins stops and grips my forearm. "We don't know who that is," he says in a low shrill voice. "It could be anyone."

"Nic?" Ria's voice echoes down the tunnel.

"Yeah! It's us!" I call out. My heart beats a little faster, suddenly finding some extra energy. "Kingston there too?"

"Who do you think had the flashlight, mate?" a male's voice answers in an island accent. "We found something. Figured you two would eventually show."

We run toward the light, reaching Kingston and Ria at the same time.

"I think we found a way out," Kingston says. He shines the flashlight up the side of the wall to show us a ladder bolted to the wall. The top disappears into the darkness.

"Whatcha think's up there?" I ask, as Kingston shines the beam back down onto the tracks between the group. It creates an eerie glow around our faces.

"Only one way to find out," Rollins says. My brother reaches for the base of the ladder. Kingston stands at the bottom and shines the light up the wall again. As soon as Rollins makes it about ten feet off the ground, the bulb starts to dim, flashes a few times, and then flutters out.

Kingston bangs his hand across the side of the flashlight. "Solar power must be drained."

I place the edge of my boot against the side of the track. The trembling has increased since we first felt the light rumble earlier. I glance over my shoulder. A very dim, distant white light emerges out of the darkness as a single speck.

My eyes grow with the dot.

"TRAIN!" I yell, pointing behind me. The spotlight continues to grow, enough to illuminate Kingston and Ria.

A strong gust of wind rushes down the tunnel.

"Everyone up the ladder, NOW!" Rollins yell.

"Ria, come on!" I reach for her hand and help her up the first couple of rungs.

She turns back. "And then you—"

A bright spotlight erupts from around the corner that illuminates the entire tunnel. The ground quakes violently, knocking me and Kingston back onto the tracks. I push myself up only to discover the left side of my boot is stuck between two grooves in the tracks.

"Kingston!" I yell, as I spot him leaping toward the ladder. "I'm stuck!"

The spotlight continues to grow; the train's getting dangerously closer. An ear piercing rumble shakes the tunnel, followed by another strong surge of wind.

76

I yank at my boot. My fingers nervously pull at my double-knotted boot strings, unsuccessfully trying to untie them.

"Kingston!" I desperately yell out again. "HELP!"

I grit my teeth and squeeze my eyes shut. Even with my eyes closed, the spotlight on the train still lights everything up.

The loud rumble gets more intense and tosses my body back and forth, like I'm standing in the middle of a hurricane.

"Nic!"

I hear a voice scream my name from above, followed by a strong telekinetic force ripping my shoe free from the track. My body shoots straight up in the air like a water fountain, and the edge of my boot nips the top of the MagneTrain as it roars past below me.

CHAPTER 16

OUTSIDERS

I'm the last one to reach the top of the ladder. My arms and legs cry out, aching worse than I've ever felt before. I release a grunt, as I push myself up the last couple of rungs and tumble onto the platform that everyone else stands on. Rollins grabs my arm and pulls me in closer to the middle of the group.

"It's a long way down, little bro. Be careful."

I twist my body around onto my stomach and hold onto the edge of the platform with my fingertips. The muscles in my arms and legs tremble. It feels like we just climbed to the highest peak of Everest. I wonder how far down the tunnel goes. I inch myself a little closer to the edge and gaze down into the dark nothingness below.

"Do we know what's above us?" I question as I stand up and back toward the center of the platform.

"No, but there's definitely something up there," Ria says. I feel her searching for my arm. We lock hands and she intertwines her fingers through mine.

"Yeah, I think I saw something in the light when the train was passing below us," Rollins answers. "Looks like a manhole cover or something. No clue what's on the other side though."

"Only one way to find out," Kingston says. He stands next to me.

All four of us direct our palms above our heads. After a moment, a circle of light begins to glow around the cover as it gradually rises up, allowing the outside light into the dark tunnel. Dirt and really fine sand cascades through the gap, falling down into our eyes and hair.

"I wonder where we ended up?" I question again out loud, as I shake some of the sand out of my hair.

"Silo," Rollins says with assurance in his voice. He wipes at his eyes. "We're so close to the station, it has to be Silo."

One at a time, my brother sends us up through the opening in the ceiling. Kingston goes first, followed by myself, Ria, and then finally Rollins raises himself up using his own power.

The bright light painfully stings my eyes as soon as I'm above ground. I'm forced to squint, unable to hold them open all the way.

"Is it always this hot in Silo?" I ask. I roll up my sleeves, instantly wishing we were still stuck down below in the tunnel where our biggest concern was the darkness…oh, and incoming trains and drones shooting at us. I guess Silo could be worse.

"Silo's just a subsector of Sol," Rollins says, as if I didn't already know. "It's the same temperature everywhere." Rollins extends his arm and drags the manhole cover back over the hole to conceal our exit. "You'll get used to it."

79

I take a look around at our surroundings. There's nothing but the same scenery I saw through the window on the train: bare, desolate land in all directions. Not a single tree or sign of anything living in sight. No matter what direction I look, it's all the same—boring, beige sand.

"Looks like Silo's just a big empty desert," Ria says.

A large patch of sand moves in the far distance. If I wasn't already gazing off in that direction, I would have probably missed it. "Look!" I exclaim, pointing toward the horizon. "Something's out there."

The sand hiccups again in the same area, this time more noticeable.

"Whatever it is, I don't wanna stick around to find out if it's friendly." Rollins holds a hand to his forehead to shade his eyes.

"So we just walk?" I question the group. "We don't even know where we are."

"Your brother already told you," Kingston says. "We're in Silo."

* * *

We walk.

And we walk.

And then we walk some more. The muscles in the back of my legs feel as tight as a stretched rubberband and I have a lump in the back of my throat that I can't swallow down. What I wouldn't do for something to drink right now.

"How do we even know we are moving in the right direction," I question for the tenth time since we started. "We could be walking right into a trap."

"Do you see anything around?" Kingston blows up. He gets in my face. "Does anything around you seem like a trap to you, mate? There's nothing out here!"

Even though I know it was rhetorical, I gaze back out into the hot sun. Little black dots dance across my vision and fall delicately into the oatmeal-colored sand in front of me, forming a structure of some kind. I blink my eyes and squint. The structure begins to grow a faint outline, but it's so far away I can't tell if it's really there.

"My eyes must be playing tricks on me," I mutter to myself. Everyone turns in the direction I'm facing. "Does anyone else see that?"

"Yeah, but what is it?" Ria questions.

Thank goodness someone else sees it.

The structure stretches out in both directions as far as I can see. It now stands out of the sand, as if it doesn't belong there, like a stranger in a new sector. Someone created whatever it is. Someone put it there. It has to be real.

"Looks like a group of buildings or something," Rollins says. My brother moves a couple of steps closer to the enormous object even though we're miles away. He holds his hand to his forehead again to shield the powerful glare of the sun.

"It's a wall," Kingston says with certainty in his voice, as if he's seen it before up close. "We're on the NoMads side of Silo. No man's land."

With little warning, the sand erupts about two hundred yards away and a long, brown-striped creature emerges from underground. Its head is serpent-like, its body flying up into the air before diving back into the sand. It's moving fast and heading straight for us.

CHAPTER 17

THE BATTLE AT THE GATE

SKRAWWW! SKRAWWW!

The giant serpent releases an ear-piercing screech just before it dives back into the sand. Its fish-like tail flaps up, allowing the lengthy beast to sweep quickly through the desert land.

All of us take a sizable step back knowing wholeheartedly we'll never be able to outrun this monster. We watch as its brown-striped head explodes out of the sand and releases another war cry. It sounds like an injured bird calling out for help.

SKRAWWW! SKRAWWW!

"Get to the Gate!" Rollins shouts. He grabs me by the arm. "RUN!"

Without question, the four of us dash across the flat desert land and head toward the structure that bizarrely wasn't even there a couple of minutes ago. I glance over my shoulder. The giant serpent continues to move across the thick sand, chasing after us.

"How do we even know they'll let us in?" Ria asks no one in particular between breaths. She stumbles, but continues running.

"One thing at a time," my brother says. The sand explodes into the air about twenty feet in front of us. A large beige cloud forms for a few seconds before being scattered by the wind.

We skid to a stop, sliding forward in the sand.

Something the size of a baseball, but black, emerges from the cloud and sails over our heads. It lands behind us and explodes upon impact, creating a crater about ten feet wide. Loud gunfire erupts behind the cloud of sand.

"NoMads!" Kingston shouts. "Get into the hole!"

We all dive into the grenade-built crater as bullets whiz erratically over our heads. Each time a gun fires, Ria's body jumps. I reach out and grab her hand. I flash a half-smile of false reassurance back at her, unsure of the outcome myself.

We all move closer to the front of the crater—the sand-built wall separating us from the NoMads.

"We're trapped," I announce the obvious. "We have NoMads shooting at us one way and some freaky serpent beast eyeing us for its next meal in the other direction."

Another grenade sails overhead and explodes, creating a new crater on the other side of our hiding place. Pounds of beige sand fly up, the desert air holding onto it for a few seconds before it rains down all around us.

"Nic's right. We have to get out of here!" Rollins says in-between rounds of shots being fired. "Sounds like they only have a few guns. Probably isn't more than a handful of NoMads over there. When the next grenade hits, we rush them." Rollins pulls a knife out of his back pocket. "It's the only way we're gonna make it to the gate."

SKRAWWW! SKRAWWW!

Just as the serpent screeches again, another grenade takes flight. It lands a few yards to the left of our hole.

"Let's move!" Rollins shouts.

We scramble out of the crater and run blindly through the cloud of sand like it's a smokescreen.

As soon as I spot something beige move in front of me, I open my palm and send the hiding NoMad shooting up in the air. With a flick of the wrist, I toss the soldier off to the side. In midair, he drops a fresh grenade in my path. I flop down on the ground and shield my face with my hands.

But the detonation never comes.

The rebel fighter didn't pull the pin out to activate it.

I stretch my arm across the ground, pulling the timed explosive over to me. I wrap my fingers around its black base. It's warm to the touch and filled with small grooves about a half inch thick carved into the surface, probably to make the weapon more aerodynamic.

I focus on the end of a rifle sticking out of the sand about twenty feet away and lock eyes with the man aiming the weapon. His face tenses up as he gets ready to fire. "Wait!" I yell.

Rollins dives into view and tackles the soldier to the ground. He wrestles away the man's gun and knocks him over the head in the process.

The surface below me hiccups. A shower of sand explodes all around me, knocking me back—and face to face with the giant serpent's head sprouting out of ground.

SKRAWWW! SKRAWWW!

The beast's head is the same length as my entire body and as thick as the four of us combined.

I freeze and sit back on my knees, paralyzed with fear. My eyes grow as its mouth opens exposing a thousand sharp, pointy teeth running up and down the inside of its jaw. A terrible stench wafts out.

"Nic, RUN!"

Its large beady eyes lock onto mine like a cobra's, reaching, almost diving toward me with a wide, open mouth. I fling myself out of the way and roll off to the side. The beast's head rears back and prepares to strike with all its strength, but it miscalculates and takes a sizable chunk out of the land instead of my body. Upset, the serpent launches back down into the sand and buries itself beneath the surface.

I take off running in the direction of the NoMads who continue to fire their weapons. I eye the gate maybe a hundred yards away, and then turn back to the rebel fighters. They're not shooting at me, they're shooting at the serpent!

The beast's head emerges from the sand. Its shifty eyes survey its surroundings as bullets bounce off of its reptilian skin that must be as thick as armor. It flicks out its long, forked tongue, before sucking it back into its mouth. That's when I notice it's not the NoMads who are firing at the snake, but Rollins, Kingston, and Ria—they have overtaken the rebel forces!

I begin running again as the serpent locates me and makes another strong lunge in my direction. I am knocked back onto the ground. Its head suspends over me as it shows me all of its razor-sharp, deadly teeth again. It lowers its head and takes a swipe at me, just as I pull the pin out of the grenade that's still grasped in my hand.

The fuse has been lit.

"Hope you enjoy eating metal!" I yell, tossing the explosive into its wide, gaping mouth.

85

The head of the beast explodes, raining down chunks of bloody carcass all over me. My face, along with the front of my ragged clothes, is now covered in red blood.

CHAPTER 18

GATEKEEPERS

I lay on my back in the blood soaked sand. My aching body is covered in thick chunks of serpent meat, yet I can't move. The blazing sun overhead begins to cook the dark red blood into my skin like I have the worst sunburn that ever existed. Every muscle in my body feels tight, tense.

A shadow pours over my face.

Rollins.

"Nic! Nic! Are you okay?" My brother's voice sounds hollow and muffled, as if he's yelling at me through a long, deep tunnel. He grabs the front of my shirt and pulls me to my feet.

I blink my eyes.

"Can you hear me, Nic?"

I nod my head and allow my mouth to fall open. "Everything sounds weird," I say. My voice doesn't even sound like my own.

"Must have been the explosion," he says, as he smears the serpent goop through my hair. A smile spreads across his face. "You just saved us! You know that, right?" His eyes shift over to the monstrous body of the striped serpent stretched out across the flat desert land. The rear section of the headless beast continues to flop around in the sand like it's still alive somehow.

I shake my head and take a deep breath, as Rollins wraps an arm around my neck and pulls me in closer to him. He immediately shoves me away playfully, like a typical older brother would do. It feels like ages since Rollins felt simply like an older brother and that's all—since things were normal and neither one of us were Teles.

I follow my brother over to the sandpit where Kingston and Ria are busily tying-up two NoMad rebel soldiers on the ground. One man is already bound, still conscious, lying on his side. His eyes move quickly around, searching for a way out. His hands are fastened to his feet, both tightly stretched behind his back. Kingston assists Ria with an unconscious prisoner, holding onto his boots while she ties a knot around his hands with a rope she got off one of the other soldiers.

Ria looks up to find me and lets the rope fall from her hands. She pushes herself up from the ground and rushes over to me, launching herself into my arms. We both fall back and Ria lands on top of me. She plants a huge kiss on my lips and strokes the side of my face, running her fingers through my blood soaked hair. A chunk of serpent meat sticks to her hand, but she doesn't care.

"My hero," she whispers, her mouth only an inch away from mine.

I lean forward and give her another kiss. We finally part, both of us matching smiles on our faces.

"Identify yourselves," a loud booming voice carries across the sand. I can't tell if the voice is a robot or human.

Ria rolls off me. Her clothes are now stained red, matching mine.

"It's the Gatekeepers," Kingston says. He holds a canteen he found in the sandpit. He squints toward the middle of the wall. The silhouettes of two dark figures stand out against the bright blue sky. They sit perched on top of the fifty foot gate protecting Silo. There's a noticeable split down the middle, showing where the gate's two doors comes together. "Not the most desirable position in the Government's Army." He sniffles and spits off to the side. "We probably gave 'em more entertainment than they've had all month."

"What do we do?" Ria asks. She takes the canteen from Kingston and tilts it back.

"Everyone stay calm and turn your Receivers on," my brother answers. He glances down at his wrist and presses a button. The screen on his Receiver lights up. "Looks like only two Keepers, we can get past them."

I stare at Kingston's bare wrist. "I think we might have a problem, but I have an idea." I move closer to the others. "How close do you think they were paying attention?"

* * *

A gust of wind blows through the pit, lifting a sheet of sand up in the air then spraying it over us. Some of it finds my blood-soaked clothes, only to add a scattered layer of beige to my otherwise red appearance. We climb out of the NoMad pit and make our way toward the gate. The closer we get to the wall, the harder the sand feels under my boots.

Our phony prisoner, Kingston, leads the way. He holds his hands securely behind his back as if they're cuffed. My brother walks behind him and grips one of the guns we found in the sandpit in his hands. Ria and I bring up the rear, marching side by side behind my brother.

"This is never gonna work," Ria mumbles low. She glances over at me. "They're gonna shoot us as soon as we open our mouths."

No one answers. I focus on the stretch of sand in front of me and try not to lose my composure. The plan has to work…what other choice do we have?

Once we get about twenty or thirty feet away from the enormous structure, another order is barked out over the loudspeakers. "Freeze and identify yourselves. You're approaching Government land."

Kingston stops, silently directing us to do the same.

"We're soldiers in the Government's Army," Rollins shouts back, loud enough to be heard over the howling wind in the distance. "We got separated from our unit when this prisoner tried to escape in a sand storm."

The two Gatekeepers continue to stare at us, refusing to discuss the information amongst themselves or turn away. Sweat runs down my face, but I'm too nervous to move and wipe it away.

"Your unit's in Silo?" one of the Keepers yells back.

Rollins nods his head. "That's what our orders said, but who knows with that giant snake out here."

"Arid Serpent," the other Keeper says. They both wear blank expressions under their dark sunglasses, giving no indication if they believe the story or not. They're dressed in desert camouflage, similar to the NoMads' uniforms, but newer looking. "They're all over NoMad territory. Never saw anyone take one out like that before though. Pretty smart."

"Thanks," I nonchalantly call out. "Can you let us in the gate so we can locate our unit and secure this prisoner?" I decide to be bold and wipe the sweat off my face. Sticky dark blood smears across my forehead, mixed with gritty sand. "And maybe a place to clean up?" I add a valiant smile to punctuate the question.

"Where are your uniforms?" the second Gatekeeper calls out. He removes the sunglasses from his face and takes a step closer to the wall's ledge.

"We were taken prisoner and stripped of our greens by some NoMads," I shout. I refuse to be intimidated and look away while lying. "We barely escaped."

The two Gatekeepers turn toward each other. One Keeper gives the other a single nod. He buys our lie.

"Approach the gate so you can be scanned," the first Keeper says, before turning away from us. He swings his gun across his back and grabs onto the ladder that's attached to the inside wall. The other Keeper widens his stance and continues to stare down at us.

Kingston lowers his head and begins to walk again, moving closer to the intersection of the steel doors in the middle of the wall. With a loud grinding sound, gears begin to turn, cracking open a single side of the door. It stretches all the way up to the ledge where the Keeper remains on guard.

"Remember, you can't let him finish the first scan," Kingston whispers. His island voice slightly shakes as the guard approaches us.

The guard who climbed down the ladder steps through the opening of the gate. He has removed his sunglasses, sliding them into his front button pocket. He approaches us holding a small black device with a red laser shooting out the front that fits in the palm of his hand.

"Looks like ya'll went through Hell to get here," the Keeper says. "What exactly happened?" He takes his eyes off of us for a second to type something into the handheld black device.

"Oh, we just escaped a Tele training base and have been running from *your* Government ever since," I say in a casual tone.

"Huh?" The man glances up from the screen and drops the scanning device to the ground. His hand reaches back to grab for his weapon, but it's too late.

CHAPTER 19

BIG HOOT'S

I jerk my hand toward the Keeper on the ground. Before he has a chance to react, I fire him backward a few yards. The back side of his head strikes the steel wall in an echoing thump. The guard's limp body slumps down a few inches and his head lolls to the side.

Kingston rushes forward and grabs the man's gun off the ground as Rollins fires a couple of shots at the guard standing above us. The Keeper raises his gun, but Ria's quicker. She spins to the side with a strong roundhouse kick in the direction of the wall. A wave of telekinetic force explodes off the end of her boot and rips the guard off of his perch. He plunges off the backside of the gate in one long scream, followed by a bone-crunching thud.

Both Keepers are now out of commission.

We cautiously enter through the open gate. One by one, we spot the guard's lifeless body on the other side of the wall. His body is mangled beyond recognition. A pool of maroon surrounds him, staining the beige sand. His gun is nowhere in sight.

Silo looks completely different than the desolate flat land right outside of the gate. Tall buildings face us directly across the paved road, dotting either side of the street leading into the subsector. Most of the buildings are in pretty good shape too, unlike back home in Sol. There are no signs of green anywhere—no plants, trees, bushes—nothing living. But that doesn't surprise me. Other than the island where the Compound is…*was*, this is what I know.

The Compound. With the nonstop craziness and running, the place hasn't really crossed my mind. All those people we left behind—Ren and August. They were…*are* Ria's friends. They became my friends. I look at Ria. She stares forward, unaware I'm looking at her. Dark bags hang under her eyes. Her short blonde bangs stick to her forehead; and her face is smeared with dirt, sand, and dark red serpent blood from when we kissed.

Three military police trucks appear around a corner in the distance, speeding down the road that leads straight to the gate. My eyes dart away from Ria and onto the approaching lead vehicle. The back of the military truck is full of uniformed soldiers from the Government's Army. We take off running in the opposite direction, with only my brother and Kingston armed with guns.

"In here!" Rollins points us toward a two-story brick building off the main road. A small electronic sign with the name, BIG HOOT'S flashes in orange over the door.

My eyes circle the inside of the establishment. The lights are dimmed, barely illuminating the dark purple velvet drapes that cover all of the windows. Round, high-top tables are scattered across the floor. Each table seats two to four people perched on barstools. Most of the patrons are soldiers of the Government's Army still in uniform. A small machine that looks like an upside-down porcelain bucket sits on top of a purple tablecloth in the center of each table. Multi-colored tubes snake out of the device and attach to the noses of those sitting at the tables. Waitresses walk around with fake smiles as they refill the multi-color tubes as soon as they reach the halfway mark, making the people stay longer.

"This is an O3 bar," Ria announces to the group. "I've heard about these places. Stuff's supposed to make you feel superhuman."

The patron's all sit with their eyes closed and heads tilted back in relaxed euphoria. The O3 drug takes them to another world.

"They gotta have a back door to this place," Rollins says, as he weaves us around the tables. "Those MP's will be here any minute."

No one seems to notice us, or our two large guns, as we make our way toward the rear of the building. We reach the back wall just as the first military truck skids to a halt in front of the bar.

"Whoa whoa whoa," a man stops us. He seems to be level headed and not under the influence. Maybe he's the owner? He has on a black T-shirt with the name and logo of the O3 bar across the front. "You can't come back here."

Rollins lifts his gun and shoves it into the man's face. "Yeah, I believe we can. You got a back exit?"

The man throws his hands up to surrender and moves to the side. He points to a hallway that leads to the back of the building.

The front door opens just as we leave the main room. Eight to ten soldiers enter the bar, lead by an officer who looks older than the rest of the men. He has a thick, dark beard and wears his hat low over his eyes. His eyes shift back and forth under the bill of his cap, scanning the room. As soon as he sees me, his eyes widen. He says something to the man standing behind him.

"Rollins—the door!" I stand frozen in the middle of the hallway. I know I should run, but my feet have forgotten how to work.

My brother snatches me by the arm and begins to drag me away. We rush down the back hallway that hooks to the right, leading us to an exit door. Rollins shoves it, but the door doesn't budge.

95

"Come on!" my brother shouts in frustration. He leans back and puts his weight into it. "It's locked," he grunts.

Kingston swings his gun across his back and aims his hand toward the center of the door.

Nothing.

We all try, one at a time, each of us with variable power.

Still nothing. The door will not open.

I hear the sound of footsteps running down the hallway. "Rollins, toss me your gun, someone's coming. You all stay back and work on the door."

Without hesitation, Rollins tosses me his gun and I take off down the hallway. I grip the weapon with both hands, the strap swinging back and forth between my legs. I skid to a stop as I reach the turn in the hallway, but not in time to keep the tip of the weapon from protruding around the corner and giving away my location. The pursing soldiers light up the already brightly-lit corridor with gunfire.

I jump as the narrowness of the hallway intensifies the sound. A row of overhead lights explodes, cloaking the hallway in darkness. The gunfire ceases for a brief second.

They must be reloading. My turn.

I lift my weapon and tilt it around the sharp corner. Blindly, I fire a round of scattered bullets. Most of them sound like they are hitting the ceiling or floor between us. I keep firing until the gun runs out of ammunition.

"Nic!" I hear Rollins call out behind me. "We got it open, let's move!

As soon as I turn to run back toward the door, a round of bullets sprays the wall only a few inches above my head. I duck and close my eyes. They're getting closer.

I sense something small fly through the air and strike the front tip of my boot, clanking onto the ground before me. I glance down and immediately know what it is.

"GRENADE!"

CHAPTER 20

MULTIPLE CHARGES

I dive to the ground and shield my face with my hands as the grenade detonates. The powerful blast lifts me a few feet into the air, before painfully dropping me back down onto the floor. A terrifyingly loud buzz invades my head as a cloud of thick gray smoke rolls over me and fills the hallway.

Am I dead?

Rollins yanks me off the floor. I can't hear anything, but I watch as my brother begins firing his gun with one hand and dragging me toward the exit with the other. The tip of his weapon emits a sharp white light every time it's fired.

I try to plant my feet underneath me, but Rollins continues to drag me across the linoleum floor so I keep losing my already shaky balance. I reach back and grab his arm.

"I'm okay!" I shout. "Let me go!"

He releases me, but my feet are unable to find level ground. I collapse against the side of the wall and fall.

My brother continues to fire over me, now holding onto the gun with both hands. He swings it back and forth like a flamethrower until the tip of his gun doesn't light up any more. He's out of ammo. All in one motion, my brother drops the useless weapon to his feet and reaches down to lift me up. He throws his arm around my shoulder and drags me away.

By the time we step out into the alley, Ria and Kingston are already outside ready to seal off the exit. Ria holds the door shut. Both of her arms are extended out before her, while Kingston lugs over a small white parked car and positions it behind the exit. Like the hallway, the alley is narrow, not much bigger than the length of the car itself. The rear side of another brick building boxes us in.

"Are you okay?" Ria questions me as soon as the door is secured. I have to read her lips to understand what she's saying. Her voice sounds muffled and confusing in my head. Her face sags down the middle, like she's worried.

"I'm okay!" I shout louder than needed. My voice finally echoes normally again through my head, putting an end to the ringing.

A loud clap of thunder cracks on the other side of the door causing me to jump. Bullets hit the inside of the door sprouting small, round dimples the size of quarters on the door's exterior.

"Doesn't look like it's gonna hold," Kingston says. He glances at the door and then around to everyone in the group. "Anyone have a plan?"

Another round of bullets strikes the interior. Fresh, new dimples pop up, encircling the handle.

"Get as far away from this place as possible?" Ria suggests the most logical plan.

Rollins nods his head. "And find our father's old lab—"

"Wherever that is," I add, as I scratch the top of my head. I fish a piece of serpent meat out of my hair and flick it onto the ground.

We start to make our way in the direction of the road when the handle to the exit door explodes off and shoots across the alley. It strikes the backside of the neighboring brick wall and falls to the ground in a ball of flames.

I glance over my shoulder as we approach the road. The top half of the rear door flies off and slams up against the opposite wall. The flaming piece of steel bounces off the building and lands in the middle of the alley. Out climbs the man with the dark beard. His cold eyes calmly observe us as we run away, not in any rush to stop us. A uniformed soldier follows him out and bends down on one knee in front of the vehicle. He balances a strange cylindrical weapon on his shoulder, about the size and length of a baseball bat. The soldier peers through a looking glass attached to the bottom of the device as he lines it up in our direction.

Boom!

The soldier pulls back on the trigger and shoots a massive neon red flaming fireball down the alley.

I dive—tackling Ria, Rollins, and Kingston onto the ground in one big sweep. The fireball races over our heads and smashes into the side of a brick building across the road. A hole twice the size of the car is left in its place. The building is engulfed in flames.

I roll off of Rollins in a cough, his hand having punched me in the stomach as we landed, knocking the breath out of me. I lie on my back and try to remember how to breathe again.

I scan the alley. The soldier with the fireball weapon is lining up another shot. I get my breath back just in time to yell, "Watch out!"

Boom!

100

A second shot roars down the alley. Rollins shoves me out of the way. The ball of fire screams by and slams into the same building as before. A crowd of panicked people rush out of the entrance, half of them surveying the damage, while others scatter off in different directions.

Kingston grabs me and yanks me to my feet. Two military vehicles screech up, each one blocking off half of the entrance at the mouth of the alley. A plethora of armed soldiers unload from the trucks.

As Kingston turns back around, he is greeted by the butt side of a gun slamming into his forehead, knocking him out cold. The same soldier flips his weapon around and shoves the barrel in my face.

I look around. Rollins and Ria have already given up. Their hands are raised over their heads.

"Nicholas McCready, you are under arrest for multiple charges. Lie down on the ground and place both of your hands behind your back. This will be your only warning."

CHAPTER 21

SWEET HOME SILO

We drive down the central road in Silo and away from the main gate's entrance and the alley behind Big Hoot's. I sit in the back seat of a military vehicle with a subdued Rollins next to me. Our wrists are handcuffed and resting before us in our laps. The counterfeit Receivers that we stole from Nox have been removed from our wrists. Ria and an unconscious Kingston were also both arrested and cuffed, and put into a matching vehicle that follows us.

I stare forward through the clear barrier that separates us from the two soldiers in the front seat. Both are males who look to be in their early twenties. They wear their hair short on the sides, almost shaved down to the scalp, with Government issued hats matching their desert camouflage uniforms. Each is equipped with a handgun on his belt and military patches line their sleeves and shirt pockets. A large weapon, identical to the one that shot fireballs at us in the alley, sits between them, locked in a holster pointing toward the roof. A radio in the front cab lights up and transmits mechanical chatter. My ears perk up when I hear our last name mentioned.

The soldier in the passenger seat reaches over to the console and presses in a flashing button. "We're on our way now with the prisoners in custody. We'll be at the gate in less than five minutes." He releases the button and relaxes back in his seat.

I turn to look out the window. A couple of blocks from the wall, the subsector really begins to open up. A big empty field filled with nothing but beige sand extends to the horizon. In the center of the large expanse stands a group of industrial-sized shiny buildings. Each structure is identical to next. A massively tall chain link fence, topped with razor-sharp barbed wire, encircles the complex. A single paved road breaks off from the main highway that we're currently on and leads up to a security gate where a sign is posted.

"Silo Government Research Base?" I mumble under my breath. My eyes bounce from one building to the next.

"This is the place," Rollins says low and confident. His words pull me away from the view out the window. "This is where Dad used to work."

Not surprisingly, we turn off the main road and head toward the gate. The driver rolls down his window as the car comes to a stop.

"We have the McCready brothers," he says. The soldier flashes an ID badge at one of the two seated guards in the gatehouse. Inside a small television plays the news, loud enough that I can almost make out the announcer's voice through the glass.

The guard closest to the window exits the small security building and holds out a pole about the length of a broomstick with a large mirror at the end. He takes his time walking around the perimeter of the truck, checking for anything illegal underneath the frame. He quickly completes his check and returns to the gatehouse, giving the two soldiers in the front seat a nod and a wave. The gate rises.

As the driver puts the vehicle in gear, I spot a bright neon light emerge from the clouds and strike the front end of our truck. Our entire vehicle soars up in the air, lifting us at least ten or fifteen feet off the ground, before crashing down awkwardly on the front end. The impact rips the front half of the vehicle free and splits the truck in half.

A loud siren sounds somewhere off in the distance. The front section of our vehicle erupts in flames.

I lie face down on the floorboard, unable to turn my head. The center of my forehead throbs, like a boulder fell on top of it. I manage to look up and discover my brother stretched out across the backseat. His eyes are closed and he has a large gash running vertically down his cheek.

Still cuffed, I push myself up just in time to spot another bright neon light strike directly behind us. The force spins the backside of our truck around to face the front of the military vehicle behind us. The truck's hood bursts into flames.

"Ria and Kingston!" I shout out. "Rollins, wake up!" I grab his arm and shake it, but I can't get him to open his eyes. A third fireball roars through the sky and hits the gatehouse, leaving a small crater in its place.

I stretch my legs out and kick the back passenger-side window as hard as I can with the sole of my boots, but it stays intact. With my wrists still locked together, I extend my arms and aim my open palms at the center of the window. A crack forms, inching its way out in all directions. A loud pop follows and the window shatters into a thousand tiny pieces.

I shimmy my way through the hole and look around. The front gate of the research base is now a warzone. My head spins. I walk around to where the front half of our vehicle used to be attached to the rest of the truck. Just like the two soldiers in the gatehouse, the driver and passenger are nowhere to be seen. They have vanished, but something is left in their place. A set of slightly charred keys lies on the ground. I reach down and grab them. I clumsily unlock my cuffs before opening the back door to free Rollins as well.

"What happened?" my brother asks weakly. He comes to as I drop the cuffs on the ground. His free hand wipes away a trail of blood trickling down his cheek.

"I think one of those fireballs hit us," I say, still feeling lightheaded. "They hit Ria and Kingston too."

His deadpan gaze studies me. Rollins shows no initial reaction to what I just told him. He reaches over and pulls a small piece of glass out of the center of my forehead, the tip stained in red. He shows it to me between his two fingers, as if it's a puzzle piece that he just discovered, before dropping it onto the ground between us.

"Ria and Kingston—are they okay?"

I jog over to the smoke-filled vehicle in flames about ten yards away. A dark shadow moves in the cab and I regain hope someone's alive.

I hobble to the backdoor of the truck just as a small hand emerges from the thick, black smoke and weakly raps against the rear driver's side window. I'm flooded with relief when I see Ria's nautical tattoo drawn across the top of the moving hand.

"Hold on Ria, I'm coming!"

I try the outside handle, but it's locked. I reach out and focus on the center of the glass again.

"Cover your face," I yell out, as the glass shatters and implodes into the rear cab. A trail of smoke escapes from the inside of the truck.

"Nic!" Ria's voice cries out faintly. She coughs and breathes in a thick cloud of smoke. Her hand protrudes out the window. She grabs onto the outside edge of the vehicle, cutting her hand on the jagged glass.

I wrap my fingers around her wrist and yank her through the opening. Kingston lies across the backseat with his eyes still closed. He releases a loud, deep cough. The entire top half of his body jumps up and his eyes spring open.

Rollins rushes to my side and together we pull Kingston through the window, freeing him from the fire and smoke.

"We get hit by a hurricane or something?" Kingston massages the top of his head where the soldier struck him with his gun. He motions toward the open gate. "At least they left the door open for us."

CHAPTER 22

KIND OF...POPULAR

Boom!

As soon as we pass through the gate, the military vehicle that we just pulled Ria and Kingston out of explodes behind us. The inflamed hood blows off the front of the truck and flies straight into the air, before gliding back down and landing harmlessly in the desert sand. All of the windows shatter, producing a high-pitched whistle, as the interior of the truck continues to burn. A continuous thick cloud of black smoke climbs out of the wreckage and swirls up into the sky.

A small group of armed soldiers rushes out of a building across the empty courtyard to investigate the explosion. We scatter and duck behind the closest building, allowing the group of soldiers to pass us.

"Who do you think fired at us?" I ask in a low whisper. Everyone is huddled together, each person on a knee.

"NoMads for sure," Rollins says with certainty. "As long as the Government is in power, there'll always be NoMad attacks." My brother ignores the group of ten soldiers who just rushed by. "Where those men just came from," he continues, as he squints toward the building's entrance, "that's where we're headed."

Another group of armed soldiers, this one much larger, exits the same building through a pair of glass doors. They jog past us in formation, each foot hitting the pavement in unison as they fall in line.

"You sure that's the place, mate?" Kingston says. His eyes follow my brother's gaze. "The place already seems kind of...popular."

My brother doesn't answer him right away. He squats down a few feet in front of us, surveying the developing scene. "It's the right place. I can feel it." He wipes away another trail of blood on his cheek. "When I say—"

Boom!

Another explosion hits the side of a building to our left and cuts my brother's plan off midsentence. Several soldiers run out of the entrance in a panic and discover us. The leader shouts a command and points at us, but it's drowned out by the shrill alarm that continues to echo across the facility.

Rollins jumps up and the rest of us follow.

Boom!

A fireball explodes into the side of the building behind us, striking the same exterior wall we were just hiding behind. The blow knocks us all to the ground and scatters our bodies across the concrete courtyard.

My vision blurs and I feel dizzy. Lying on my side, I can't raise my head up more than a few inches. I feel like I'm in quicksand, paralyzed from the neck down. How many times can one person get blown up in a day? I try to locate Ria or even Rollins, but all I can see is a bunch of sideways boots rushing toward me.

I blink my eyes and attempt to guess how many soldiers are approaching, but I immediately give-up when I realize I'm actually seeing double. There's far too many and I don't have the strength to hold them all off by myself. I roll onto my back and stare up at the sky. The back of my head aches.

Boom!

Another explosion strikes a building located somewhere else on the complex and lights up the sky. The ground angrily rumbles beneath me. I try to push myself up, but a hand knocks me right back down. A soldier has launched himself on top of me. The palm of his hand strikes me underneath my chin and jerks my head back in pain. He flips me over, cuffs my hands together behind my back, and then uses my body to push himself up.

"You're under arrest McCready, now stay down!" He unleashes a series of kicks into my side.

I let out a gasp, choking back the pain. My eyes search the ground. Amongst all the burning buildings and a few soldiers lying on the ground dead, I spot three other figures on the opposite side of me. All three lie still on their stomachs, their hands also cuffed behind their backs.

"All four terrorists have been apprehended," a booming voice calls over me, loud enough to make out even over the alarm. "We're bringing them in—"

Boom! Boom!

Two more explosions strike back to back, followed by gunshots rattling across the courtyard. Uniformed soldiers begin to drop to the ground.

"What's going on?" Ria shouts. She lays a few feet away from me. The sound of used bullet casings continues to clatter all around us. "Are they shooting each other?"

Eventually the surprise attack is over and the only thing I can hear is the alarm as it continues to blare.

CHAPTER 23

THE CHOICE IS YOURS

"On your feet, boy," a scratchy, deep voice orders me up. I feel a pair of hands grab me by the cuffs and yank me up.

A soldier dressed in an unusual navy blue uniform stands a few yards away. He holds a large gun with both hands and sports a crooked smile on his face, as if I'm his trophy. I spy two other soldiers, both in matching desert camouflage, lift Ria and the others up, one by one. Even though the two men wear the same color of camo, the uniforms have been altered differently. One soldier has his sleeves cut off, while the other wears multiple patches and a strange flag on his shirt.

"This way," the soldier in blue threatens us. He shoves his gun toward the group. "Inside!"

We are marched toward the entrance of the lab, the same building we were trying to reach earlier. Both doors are held open by uniformed soldiers—one dressed in altered desert camo, while the other wears navy blue.

111

The first thing I notice as I cross the threshold is the temperature of the room we enter. The air conditioning is cranked up so high it feels like winter. The lights are dimmed low, but I am able to make out a few unconscious bodies wearing white lab coats and desert camouflage sprawled out across the floor.

"The McCready brothers," a woman announces to no one in particular. She turns to face us, but remains on the far side of the room cloaked in shadow. She holds a tablet in her hands that's flashing something across the screen. Her wrists are bare, matching the Receiver-less soldiers outside. "Please have a seat. With everything you've been through, I know you're exhausted." She pauses and extends her hand in a casual way. "We've been expecting you since you escaped the Compound."

My breath catches at the mere mention of the training facility. My knees feel like they're about to buckle, but out of principle I refuse to sit. Silently, everyone follows my lead and declines the chairs behind us.

The woman slithers out of the shadows and moves almost directly under a spotlight after stepping over several bodies. The bright overhead light creates deep shadows on her face, conveying the evil intimidation her voice alone doesn't accomplish.

"Did you not hear the minister?" the soldier in all blue bellows behind me. He shoves me down into a chair using only one hand. Three other chairs remain empty next to mine in a row.

One by one, starting with my brother, the others take a seat.

"Now that we got that out of the way, please let me introduce myself. I am Prime Minister Tess Savron," the woman says. She pauses to peer at us like we should be impressed. After an uncomfortable few seconds, she gives up waiting on a response. "I am the leader of the free rebels, who you and others refer to as the NoMads. We do not fight for any Government, but for ourselves, to better this country."

I study the woman's face. I recognize little details about her—the small scar running vertically down between her eyes; the tip of the blue tattoo just peaking out of her buttoned-up collar; the way she parts her hair down the middle and dresses in old fashion clothes—this is the woman who appeared on the screens back at the Compound before the bombs hit. How could she have known we escaped?

"We don't fight for this country either, mate," Kingston growls as he cuts off the prime minister. "So you can let us go."

"Oh we are fully aware who each of you are," the woman says, and then to prove her point she adds the name, "Kingston." She moves away from the spotlight and approaches the area where we remain seated. "This is why I request your help today."

I glance over at Rollins, only to have my head yanked back around by the soldier standing behind me. "Pay attention when the minister is talking to you."

"There's no need for that," Prime Minister Savron calmly says. Her voice is unsteady like she doesn't even believe her own words. "They'll comply." She nods her head, convincing herself. "What other choice do they have?" She forces a brief smile.

"We are fully aware of your task at hand; the one that Dr. Max Dreadnought requested you to fulfill?" She says it like a question, as if she's unsure, but she must know something about the flash drive. "We're here to assist you in completing your mission."

"What's the catch?" Rollins says. The prime minister glares at him. "Why would you help us?"

"Like your friend said," the woman begins, "we're on the same side." She sits down, now only a few yards away, and crosses her legs. Her full-length black skirt hikes up a few inches so we can see the tops of her leather boots. She brings her hands together, intertwining her fingers in her lap.

In the shadows behind Minister Savron, I spot the back end of what looks like a Healer. It must be the Transporter. Rollins was right.

"We're going to send you four back in time to end the Tele program before it can begin," Minister Savron says. She closes her mouth for a second as if she has completed her statement, but then opens it again to add, "And to install the program on this flash drive onto any Government computer. It's as simple as that." She pulls a miniature flash drive out of her pocket and holds it out to show us.

"What's on the drive?" I speak up.

"That's none of your concern," Minister Savron snaps back. She exhales and gets up from her seat as if she's disappointed that I would ask such an annoying question. She approaches the Transporter behind her, delicately running her fingers all the way down the side of the device, before slapping the end of it. Her open palm releases a loud pop that echoes off of the metal cover. "You can either accept our assistance or, sadly, your mission will end here. The choice is yours."

CHAPTER 24

TRANSPORTER

Before Rollins can volunteer, I shoot out of my chair. "Send me first!" This time the soldier in blue doesn't force me back down. He allows me to approach the minister and the Transporter.

"Excellent," Prime Minister Savron says. The hint of a smile grows on her face. She grabs a radio off the ledge behind her and holds it to her mouth. "We're ready. Send out our assistant." She picks up a black vest with a lightning bolt embossed across the front and holds it out in front of her. "Put this on underneath your shirt and do not remove it under any circumstances." She hands me the vest.

In the time it takes for me to strap it on, two men appear in the doorway on the far side of the lab. One is an armed soldier dressed in the same navy blue uniform the guard standing behind my chair is wearing. He holds his gun to the back of a second man whose face is hidden in the shadows.

"We wouldn't want anything to happen to our precious cargo, so we enlisted a former employee that you may be familiar with," Savron says. The smile on her face grows with her voice. Let me reintroduce you to Dr. Max Dreadnought. I believe he was your father's colleague?"

Dr. Dreadnought is escorted out of the shadows and placed under a spotlight. The soldier releases him and takes a sizable step back. His gun remains pointed at the doctor.

"This is insane," Dr. Dreadnought mutters under his breath. He shakes his head to the side in short movements and refuses to look up.

"Excuse me?" Savron asks the doctor. "Did you say something, Dreadnought?" She walks the short distance across the floor to the other side of the Transporter. The bottom of her boots click, echoing, as she makes her way across the tile.

"We don't even know if it's safe for humans yet," Dr. Dreadnought says with a low voice. He keeps his eyes on the floor. "We've only tested non-living objects and some small animals so far. We haven't even tried sending a mammal yet."

The prime minister nods her head as she runs her fingers across the top of the Transporter, the same way as before, guiding her way to the other side of the device. Dr. Dreadnought finally looks up. His eyes find mine.

"That didn't stop you from ordering these kids to use this machine on their own." The minister glances back at me with a fake concerned look. "And we have such a brave volunteer who's so eager to be the first time traveler in history!" Her voice rises with excitement. "Come forward, Nicholas McCready." She raises a hand like she's a Tele getting ready to move an object with her mind, directing me to move closer.

I glance over to the others. Rollins starts to push himself up, but the soldier in blue knocks him back down with the same force he did to me moments ago. "I'll be right behind you, little bro!" Rollins jerks back his elbow and frees his shoulder from the soldier's firm grip.

I nod my head, accepting my fate and inch closer to the device. I climb into the Transporter and lie down on my back. I cross my arms over my chest, just like the man in the video, and stare at the ceiling. Prime Minister Savron moves into my view. She holds the flash drive between two fingers.

"Since the Transporter did not exist in the time period you are about to enter, you will need us to bring you back. In order for this to happen, you must install this program onto a Government computer. We will know when this happens." She stuffs the drive into the palm of my hand, wrapping my fingers around it. "Good luck, young man."

The lid closes over me, abruptly ending any chance I have of calling off this crazy plan. It's pitch black for about twenty seconds before a thin blue light forms, running around the circumference of the interior of the coffin-like box. The blue light begins to grow brighter and brighter all around me, so bright I have to shut my eyes. A loud clicking noise begins behind my head as the light continues to grow even more intense. I squeeze the flash drive in my hand, my fingers almost crushing the small rectangular piece of plastic.

And then, just like that, everything stops. The blue light vanishes, along with the loud clicking noise.

Everything is still and feels the same.

I guess it didn't work.

I open my eyes and discover a plain white ceiling above me. I quickly realize I'm not in the Transporter anymore...nor the present.

I have successfully traveled back in time.

CHAPTER 25

THE WHITE ROOM

One by one, the others begin to show. First my brother, followed by Ria, and then Kingston. All four of us stare at each other in the empty white room, confused.

"At least we're all together, but where are we?" I break the silence. My eyes bounce around the room. There are no windows looking outside, only a door in the center of a wall with a small window cut out. The only thing I can see on the other side of the door is another plain white wall.

"Or even better yet, *when* are we?" Ria answers my question by adding one of her own. "Who knows what time period that psycho sent us back to."

Rollins paces back and forth underneath the bright fluorescent lights running across the low ceiling. Kingston sits on the ground in one of the corners of the room with his elbows resting on his bent knees.

"Seems to be some kind of cell." Rollins stops and glances back at the group. "What I don't understand is why this isn't a lab.

Savron sent us back in time, not to a different location." My brother starts pacing again after no one comments.

"Maybe that Dreadnought guy altered something," Kingston chimes in after a hard minute of silence. He straightens his legs on the floor. "Maybe he was trying to protect us?"

"Or he did something so we wouldn't succeed in carrying out the NoMads' plan," I add, as my eyes follow Rollins across the small room. "But how else will we get back?" The prime minister's flash drive is still locked in the palm of my hand. I slide it into my front pocket knowing it is our ticket home.

Outside, a dark shadow crosses by the small window. Within seconds, it returns and unlocks the door. Kingston pops up off the ground at the sound of the door opening.

A man stands in the doorway, dressed in a navy blue military uniform, matching the two soldiers from the future—our present. He is in his early thirties with dark brown hair and gray eyes. His uniform is covered in military patches and the bottom edge of a large upper arm tattoo sneaks out from under his right sleeve.

"What are you guys doing in here?" the man questions. He leaves the door open behind him and cautiously steps into the center of the cell. "No one's supposed to be in here until tomorrow." His eyes fall on me. "What happened to you?"

I look down at my hands, forgetting that they are still covered in serpent blood, along with my arms, face, and clothes. "We were arrested outside of the gates for poaching and taken here."

"Gates?" The soldier's eyes leave me and shift over to Rollins. He reaches back for the gun around his belt. He doesn't remove it from the holster, but his hand doesn't leave the top of the weapon either.

"It surrounds Silo," Rollins quickly adds. "But we're not supposed to be here. There was some kind of mistake."

119

The soldier digests the information. "Wait, what's she doing in here? Female inmates are held on the opposite end of the prison."

The soldier pulls his gun, but my brother is faster. Rollins extends his hand and rips the pistol right out of the man's grip before he can even get his index finger on the trigger. The gun darts across the short distance of the cell, straight into my brother's waiting hand.

The soldier's eyes widen. He turns for the open door just as I slam it shut from across the cell. Rollins lifts the gun and aims it at the back of his head.

"Not so fast," Rollins shouts. He motions the weapon away from the door. "Up against the wall."

The man makes his way toward the rear of the cell. He presses his back against the wall as instructed. "You're never gonna get away with this, you...what are you?" The idea of someone moving objects with their mind is completely foreign to him or anyone else in this time period. Teles did not exist in this world.

"Don't worry about us, mate," Kingston says as he unhooks the large ring of keys from the man's belt. "I don't think you'll be needing these anymore." Kingston twirls the keychain around on his index finger mockingly in front of the man's face.

Rollins slowly approaches the man. "What do you know about Dr. Josiah McCready? What section of the prison does he work in?"

The soldier in blue keeps silent and continues to stare at the floor.

"There are ways to make him talk," Kingston announces. He cracks his knuckles, threatening the soldier. Kingston grabs the front of the man's shirt.

"Never heard of him!" the soldier shouts. He still refuses to make eye contact with anyone, especially Kingston.

"Worthless," Kingston mutters. He releases him and, in one motion, roughly shoves the soldier back against the wall.

"He's not at this facility, I can tell you that." The soldier's voice sounds subdued and weak.

"I thought you said Dad was here?" I question my brother. "I thought he worked here?"

Rollins lets his arm relax and drops the gun to his side. He tucks the tip of the weapon into the back of his waist. "Maybe we're in a time before he worked here?" His head tilts slightly to the side as he ponders his own theory.

"Wait, what?" The soldier perks up. "What are you talking about? Time?"

The four of us leave the room and the confused soldier without another word. Kingston closes and locks the door behind us.

"Looks like we're heading back to Sol," Rollins says as he leads us down the narrow hallway. "Not sure where else to look."

CHAPTER 26

YOU SMELL LIKE SERPENT

As soon as we exit the cell, a camera attached to the wall finds us—an ominous, tiny red blinking dot coming from the end of the hallway. Kingston raises his hand and pulls the security camera off the wall and smashes it on the ground.

Rollins stops and turns around with a grave look. "Don't use telekinesis unless it's the last resort. Treat it like a powerful weapon."

A door on the opposite end of the hall rattles opens. We duck into an open doorless hallway off to the side.

We stand completely still up against the neighboring wall and listen to multiple boots clicking and clacking across the cement floor behind us. The noise stops as it reaches the opposite side of our wall.

"What happened here?" a male's voice asks.

"You gonna call it in?" another voice questions.

Rollins stands closest to the hall's entrance with me and Ria next to him, followed by Kingston. My brother points around the corner, holding up all five fingers. He nods his head, craning it toward the hall and begins to count down to zero on his hand.

"Control, this is 149, it looks like—"

Once Rollins runs out of fingers and makes a fist, he nods again, and jumps out from around the corner. We follow, tackling the two surprised soldiers to the ground. The handheld radio flies out of the guard's grasp and slides a few feet away.

Kingston rolls around on the floor wrestling one of the guards. The soldier is able to get a solid punch in under Kingston's chin, knocking him back. The man scrambles to push himself up and eyes the door on the opposite end of the hallway. Ria turns around just in time to spot the man as he attempts to escape. She raises her fist and jabs a wave of telekinetic force in his direction. The barrage of punches throws him hard against the wall. His body crashes forward, burying his face into the ground. He's out cold.

The other guard, the bigger of the two, rips himself away from my brother and me. He pushes himself off the floor and dives for the loose radio. He wraps his fingers around it and pushes in the transmission button.

"Control!"

Rollins grunts and flips himself around. He draws the pistol from his waistband and points it at the guard. "STOP!"

The guard freezes and raises his hands over his head.

"Tell whoever's on the other end that it was a false alarm. One of the cameras fell and that you'll contact maintenance yourself."

The guard stares at my brother, pondering his instructions. "You know you're never going to get away," he says with no sign of hope in his voice.

"So we have been told," Rollins answers. "Say it!" He inches closer to the man.

The guard presses in the transmission button again and repeats what my brother instructed him to say. He then bends down and gently places the radio on the ground, careful not to break it.

"10-4, 149," the radio buzzes back. The tiny green bulb glows as the voice comes through the speaker.

"Nic, grab that other guard and drag him into the side hall," Rollins says. "You," he says, speaking to the conscious guard who remains standing with his arms raised over his head, "this way."

We quickly realize that the adjacent hallway is not actually a hallway. It's the guards' locker room, equipped with full lockers lining the walls and a small bathroom with numerous shower heads to clean up after a shift.

"Get us some uniforms," Rollins orders the guard. He trains the pistol at him. "We're gonna walk right outta here like we own the place." He smiles, reminding me of back when he used to play baseball growing up and would always win. Rollins was always so sure of himself.

"How close is the nearest train station?" I question the guard.

"The station?" the man answers, looking at me. He raises an eyebrow. "The train station hasn't been operational since the war." His head cocks to the side. "What's going on here?"

Rollins lifts the gun and cuts the guard off. "Nic, get in the shower. You're starting to smell like serpent. Go clean up."

"Serpent?" the guard asks. His confused stare rolls over all four of us.

"Another time, another place, mate," Kingston says with a laugh. He slaps me on the back as I pass.

I lift my blood-stained shirt off over my head and look down. The Transporter vest is still strapped over my chest.

Ria starts to follow me, but Rollins lifts his hand, holding her back.

"I don't think so, Ria," he says still smiling. "We really don't have a lot of time here."

I glance back over my shoulder and match the guilty smile she's wearing before entering the showers solo.

* * *

After everyone has showered and changed into clean navy blue guard uniforms with matching hats, we take both the conscious and unconscious guards into our old cell and lock them up with the other hallway guard who tried to radio in earlier. The hallway is now clear.

Silently, we creep down empty hallway after empty hallway, all of them identical to the one before. Security cameras blink back at us, but in uniform, we're doing exactly what my brother said we would do—walk out like we own the place.

We approach a security checkpoint that could be an exit. Ria walks in front of me, her blonde hair tucked up under her blue camouflaged hat. My eyes glide down her back, moving all the way down to her boots. Even in uniform she's gorgeous.

I meet Ria's troubled eyes as she glances back over her shoulder. Two soldiers stand at the opposite end of the hallway checking the IDs of a handful of soldiers in line to exit the facility.

Rollins, who is in the lead, turns back with the same look of concern.

"Remember when I said only use your powers when it's an emergency?" He doesn't wait for a response. "Now's the time."

Without warning, Rollins pulls the gun out of his holster and fires three bullets into the ceiling.

CHAPTER 27

BACK TO THE DESERT

Rollins rushes forward and violently shoves his way past the guards waiting in line, knocking the first two to the ground. My brother sweeps the gun through the air and drives back the two soldiers checking IDs. One reaches for the gun holstered on his belt, but quickly removes his hand as Rollins hurries toward him.

On the opposite side of the security checkpoint, the sound of the echoing gunshots makes two soldiers duck down behind a waist-high barrier, along with a guard who is attempting to enter the prison. A single walk-through metal detector sits unoccupied at the entrance.

Rollins grabs the soldier who's still holding onto a thumb scanner and wraps an arm around his neck, pulling him closer. "No one try to stop us, or I'll shoot." My brother holds the pistol to the side of the man's head. His index finger rests on the trigger.

Shots ring out from the other side of the security checkpoint. One of the soldiers lowers the gun after firing. I reach out and yank the weapon out of the man's hand. His eyes widen, unable to compute what he's witnessing. Dumbfounded, he watches his pistol fly through the air and land straight into my waiting hand.

I grab Ria by the shirt sleeve. Her feet are stuck to the ground, as if she's standing in wet cement, and I begin to drag her forward. Kingston is already behind Rollins pushing his way through the gate.

"Back up!" Rollins screams. He propels himself through the checkpoint with his prisoner still locked in his grasp. "Get down on the ground!"

The lone free soldier on the other side of the exit, along with the other guards who were in line trying to leave, all join the guard lying down on the floor.

"You two over there," I call across the room as I step over the people scattered across the floor. "Toss your guns over here."

The two soldiers slide their pistols a few feet across the floor, neither of them reaching us. Ria and Kingston grab both weapons off the ground. Kingston reaches into the holster of the soldier who remains on the floor and disarms him as well. He puts the extra gun in his waistband.

"Now, we're gonna leave before anyone gets hurt," Rollins says. He scans the room and tightens the grip around the soldier's neck as the man tries to squirm out of his headlock. The man releases a choking grunt. "Everyone understand?"

No one responds, but now weaponless, they have no chance of stopping us anyway.

We make it to the door and then it hits me. I turn back and find one of the soldiers on the ground holding a live radio to his mouth. He spots me, knowing he's caught, but it's too late. He finishes the transmission anyway.

"They're at the exit now!" he calls, loud enough now for everyone in the room to hear. "We need backup!"

We rush through the exit door and meet the bright desert sun overhead.

"We need a vehicle," my brother says. He shoves the soldier down on the ground and stands over him as the defenseless man tries to muster up a response. Rollins squats and presses the gun under the soldier's chin. My brother's eyes light up as he grits his teeth.

The man closes his eyes and points in the direction of a large parking lot. Almost every spot is filled with identical off-road, military trucks. All of them are painted in the same desert camouflage, similar to the ones we were riding in to the Silo Research Base, before the NoMads blew it up.

We leave the weaponless soldier on the ground and the four of us sprint across the entrance of the prison that leads to the parking lot. Rollins yanks on the first door handle he reaches and pulls open the driver's side door.

"Keys!" he shouts, shocked that they're hanging from the ignition.

We climb inside and Rollins cranks up the engine. Kingston races around to the front passenger's side door and jumps in just as a series of shots are fired at us.

The glass from the back window shatters into the back of the cab.

"Go! Go! Go!" Kingston shouts.

Rollins jerks the vehicle out of the space and through the large parking lot, heading toward the main gate that separates the subsector and the desert.

CHAPTER 28

KILLSWITCH ENGAGE

"They're still building the wall," I say, pointing out the obvious. I lean forward between the two front seats and check out the scene through the front windshield. Men dressed in military navy blue uniforms are busy constructing part of the wall where the future gate will connect. Cranes swing large pieces of steel toward the structure on either side of the road, far from completing the laborious project.

The paved road turns into dirt as we cross through the construction site. A few soldiers glance over as we pass, but no one stops us since we're in a military vehicle with darkly tinted windows.

"Does this highway take us all the way to Sol?" I ask. I turn my attention to Rollins as he continues to drive, putting the partially constructed wall behind us.

"You know as much as me, little bro." He grips the wheel, but takes his eyes off the road for a second to meet my stare through the rearview mirror. "We'll take it as far as it'll go."

We race over one of the few hills in our path on the narrow two-lane highway that heads west toward the setting sun.

* * *

"What's going on?" Rollins shouts. The vehicle begins to decrease in speed on its own. We have been driving down the main dirt road with the same scenery for the past twenty or thirty minutes.

"Out of gas?" Kingston questions. He leans over to check the gauge on the dash.

"Nope." Rollins shakes his head. He taps the gas gauge with the tip of his index finger. "Everything looks fine." He yanks the wheel to the right and pulls the truck over to the side of the road as it rolls to a stop. The interior lights blink and sputter a few times, before finally fading out.

"Either the battery's dead," Kingston says, as he glances back at me and Ria, "or they just hit the killswitch." He opens the front passenger side door. "Bad news for us either way."

We check the vehicle for supplies before ditching it. I find a single jug of water in a hidden, rear compartment behind our seat.

"Better than nothing," I say. I hold up the water to show everyone.

Rollins nods his head in approval, before leading us off on a hike into the desert for the second time today.

* * *

I can feel a change in the weather since the sun started setting. The temperature has slightly dropped, indicating it's probably going to get pretty cold once nightfall hits.

I take a swig from the water jug and offer it over to Ria, who also takes a sip. "Guys?" I say to Rollins and Kingston, tipping the jug forward.

"We're good," my brother answers for both of them by holding up his hand. "We need to conserve as much water as we can." He doesn't turn around to face me, but I can hear a slight change in his voice; a different tone. He talks to me like I'm a little, annoying kid. "We don't know how far away we are from the border."

"Especially now since we have to stay off the main road," Kingston adds.

"Let's face it," Ria says, "once they send out a drone searching for us, we're toast." She says what everyone else is thinking, but doesn't want to admit.

"Not if we reach Sol first," Kingston answers with some energy in his voice.

"How do we even know what condition Sol's gonna be in post-war?" I call out to no one in particular. I take another small gulp and put the cap back on the water jug and eye the remaining level at about half-full. "And—"

"We know as much as you know, Nic!" my brother snaps. "We don't know anything!" He takes a few more steps and releases a long exhale. The brief moment of awkward silence is overtaken by the sound of our boots crunching across the sand. "Why don't you save your breath, little bro." His voice relaxes a little bit, lowered as if in defeat. "I have a feeling we have a long walk ahead of us."

"What's that?" Ria says. She freezes next to me and grabs my arm. Using her free hand, she points forward. A growing black dot jumps over a hill, far off in the distance.

"NoMads?" I question. My eyes drift over to my brother for an answer before landing back on what seems to be some kind of off-road vehicle.

"The only people who know we're out here are the Government's Army of Silo," Rollins says. "Don't pull any weapons until I give the sign."

A dune buggy races up to us. The driver rips the wheel to the side and hooks the car sideways. The body of the shiny, all-black vehicle now blocks our path. The driver climbs out of the front seat; his dark gear matches his vehicle's paint job. He wears a motorcycle helmet with a tinted visor across the front, reminding me of the helmets the Compound used to restrain their incoming recruits. A black leather jacket, pants, and a pair of dark boots completes the mysterious man's outfit.

"What's the sign?" I lower my voice, questioning my brother a few feet in front of me.

"Let's just see what he wants," Rollins says. He's careful not to take his eyes off the approaching man. His fingers grip the handle of the gun stuffed behind in his waistline. "He doesn't look like a NoMad or part of the Government's Army."

The man flips his visor up and reaches a hand into one of his front pockets.

"Hold it right there!" Rollins says, as he draws his gun. The rest of the group mimics my brother.

"Whoa, whoa, whoa!" the man shouts. He pulls his hand out of the pocket holding a folded piece of white paper. He slightly raises his hands before him, both barely over his head. "I'm just looking for some verification—just checking to see if I got the right people." He pries the helmet off his head. His long brown hair falls to his shoulders and blows slightly in the desert wind.

"And who's that, mate?" Kingston asks. He takes a couple of steps forward and matches my brother's wide stance.

"I'm looking for the McCready brothers." From ten feet away, the man holds up a piece of paper with both of our photos on it.

CHAPTER 29

NOSE DEEP

"And I think that's you two, right?"

Out of the corner of my eye, I steal a glance over at Rollins. He glares at the man in black standing before us, refusing to answer the question.

"I guess I should have introduced myself first." The man takes a small step forward only to immediately recoil when Rollins pulls back the slide of his gun.

The man nods his head a couple of times comprehending the situation, all while still holding his hands in the air. He's thin but with some muscle tone and his skin is a perfect golden color, just like a Greek god.

"The name's Riley Sanders. I work for Dr. Max Dreadnought," he lowers his voice even though we're the only people in sight, "in the future…you know, the present?" He drops his hand that's holding onto the sheet of paper down to eye level to read something off the back. "He told me to meet you in Silo. Said you would need a distraction and possibly an escape route out of the subsector. I just didn't think we'd be meeting in the middle of the desert." A sliver of a smile shows itself for a split second before vanishing. "He sent me back to assist you in the mission."

"Which one, mate?" The expression on Kingston's face does not change the slightest. His cold, hard stare practically burns a hole through the man's dark leather clothes.

"Which one, what?" Riley asks confused, as he continues to hold a single raised hand in the air.

"Which mission did Dreadnought send you on to assist?" Rollins joins in on the interrogation.

Riley glances down at the printout in his hand one more time before looking back up. He raises his left eyebrow over the tip of his thin wire-rimmed glasses. "To end the Tele program?"

"You could have gotten those photos from anywhere off of GovtNet," Kingston continues. The tone of his voice is icy like his glare. "How do we know you're not part of the NoMads?"

"I'll check him for weapons," Rollins says. My brother steps forward, not waiting to ask the man for permission. He pats him down, but does not find anything. "He's clean."

"Who comes out here without a weapon?" Ria questions low, only intended for me to hear.

"A mid-level lab tech from the future," Riley answers. His eyes find Ria standing next to me. "Guns don't transfer properly through a Transporter. Dr. Dreadnought saw to that."

Rollins makes eye contact with everyone as he steps away from the man and rejoins the group. "Why wouldn't Dreadnought tell us about you?"

"That I don't know." Riley considers the question for another second or two. "Maybe if you were caught, you'd know less?" He shrugs his shoulders. "Either way, if you're on foot, someone can't be too far behind you. We need to get out of here."

136

Just the tip of the sun shows over the horizon now, producing a long dark shadow that blankets over the sand. Nightfall will be here any minute. In the distance, a small light is moving across the desert shadow and away from the dropping sun.

"What's that?" I ask, pointing toward the horizon.

Riley stares off in the same direction as everyone else. "NoMads?" he answers with panic in his voice. "We need to leave now. You don't want to be here to find out if they're friendly or not."

Suddenly, an aerial drone rips through a group of clouds and launches a missile at the unaware vehicle. The strike hits its target and the vehicle explodes in a large fireball.

"Is that enough to convince you?" Riley says sarcastically. He slides his open-visor helmet back over his head. "Get in." He climbs back into the driver's seat and pulls the steel safety frame down over his seat.

"Come on," Rollins says, making the decision for the group. "Our guns won't protect us from a Hawk."

We chase Rollins over to the buggy and the four of us climb into the cab. Riley pulls down the steel outer frame that stretches across the entire vehicle, securing us in. As soon as the safety bars click into place, he hits the gas, spraying sand from the rear wheels. We take off in the same direction he came from moments ago as the aerial drone approaches us overhead.

"Don't worry," Riley's voice comes on over the rear cab's speakers, "this isn't some ordinary desert vehicle. We can defend ourselves."

Our driver opens a small compartment on the front dash that holds a single red button. Once the drone moves in front of us, Riley pushes in the button and two outer hidden doors just above the rear wheels open. Two missiles protrude out from the openings and tilt back at a ninety degree angle.

A soft beeping sound emits over the rear speakers. As the drone gets closer, the speed and volume of the beeping increases.

Riley flips down a switch located next to the steering wheel and launches a single missile into the air. The drone weaves around the incoming rocket and dodges the attack. It releases a barrage of its own gunfire as it passes over us.

Riley slams on the brakes and spins the base of the vehicle around so we're now facing the opposite direction. The drone continues across the sky. Riley lines us up with the target and fires off the second missile as the aerial drone turns around. The drone meets our surprise attack head on, and is knocked out of the sky. It loses all power and falls, plowing headfirst into the sand.

"And that's how it's done folks," Riley says. He follows the statement with an excited, loud war cry, like he just defeated the entire drone program.

"Wow, I thought it would have been a bigger explosion," I say. My eyes study the downed aircraft.

As Riley turns the buggy's wheel sharply back around onto the makeshift road, a fiery explosion erupts behind us.

Boom!

"Something a little more like that?" Riley questions with his eyebrows raised. He pauses for a response. "Next stop, Sol!"

CHAPTER 30

SAFE HOUSE

"What're they doing?" Ria asks, as our vehicle races down the main road of Sol.

We drive by several buildings with lines of people trailing out of the main doors and into the street. Official looking banners hang down the sides of the tall structures, each with the word REGISTRATION printed on top, followed by different letters of the alphabet.

"All post-war citizens are required to register with the Government," Riley's voice comes on over the cab's speakers. "They're getting fitted for Receivers."

I make brief eye contact with a young child who's waiting in a line that snakes out onto the edge of the road. He loosely holds onto his mother's hand as she peers toward the front of the building. She scratches at the side of her dirt-covered face before moving her hand down the side of her neck. Her long, graying dark hair is a matted mess. Like the majority of the people in line, the mother and son are dressed in dirty, tattered clothes. The boy watches as we pass, following the back of our buggy until we go over a small hill and I lose sight of him.

"In exchange for registering with the Government, they're given food and housing," Riley continues. "There's not enough food and supplies for everyone, so those chosen are given a date and location to report to. For some of them, it's their only chance of survival."

"Sounds a lot like Nazi Germany," Rollins says low, under his breath. His eyes glare out the window behind me, studying random faces as we roar past. "Do they tattoo them too?"

I turn toward my brother. He's right. We're witnessing the beginning of the end here. My eyes wander back out the window. We pass an electronic billboard with my last name scrolling across the front. A video plays of a young man with dark hair dressed in a white lab coat. He stands behind a podium and addresses a crowd. We turn onto the next road before I can figure out what the sign is advertising.

And then it hits me. My eyes grow large. "Was that...?"

"Your father on the billboard?" Riley's confirming voice answers over the speakers. "Once we get to the safe house, I'll explain everything."

We take the next road on the left and enter a run-down neighborhood that looks only partially occupied. Riley pulls the dune buggy into a short, narrow driveway that leads up to a garage attached to a single-story brick house. The garage door opens as we approach the house, letting us in.

* * *

The only pieces of furniture in the living room are two battered couches that don't match. No light enters the room from outside; the windows are boarded up with thin sheets of metal blocking out the outside world.

Riley flips a switch to a small generator sitting in the living room and cranks up the engine. A couple of scattered lamps light up across the room creating a warm glow.

"Home sweet home," he says sarcastically, as he walks into the kitchen. Riley opens the refrigerator door and peers inside. "There are a couple of beds in the back. I suggest everyone gets some rest before we go over the mission in detail. You know, clear your head."

"We're not going anywhere until we get some answers," Kingston says. He steps around my brother. "You think we've made it this far by trusting people? What is this place?"

Riley pops his head over the narrow bar that separates the kitchen from the living room. "I'm not sure what else I need to do to earn your trust, but did I not just save you back there in the desert? You think the Government's Army or whoever that was coming for us, would just ask you a few questions and send you on your way?" He tosses a handful of Nutribars onto the bar, along with four unmarked glass bottles of some kind of dark liquid, and pops the tops off of each one with a bottle opener. "Like I said before, this is a safe house. You're okay here."

"We'll sleep in shifts," Rollins says, turning back to the group. He grabs a Nutribar and peels back the wrapper. "Nic you stay out here with me. Ria and Kingston—try and get some rest. We'll go over everything in a couple of hours once we can all think straight. I need to talk to my brother."

"You really think I'm gonna sleep at a time like this, mate? We're here to do a job, so let's figure out a plan and get back to the right time period."

One at a time everyone else follows my brother's lead and grabs a Nutribar. My stomach rumbles at the thought of food. I peel off the top of the wrapper and take a large bite.

141

Ria nods her head, agreeing with Kingston that she's not going anywhere.

"Fine, let's talk." Rollins picks up one of the clear, dark bottles. He raises the oval opening to his nose and sniffs it. He shrugs his shoulders and takes a swig. "What is this?"

"Root beer," Riley says. He walks around the bar holding an open bottle in his hand. "The water here is unsafe to drink. This is all I could get." He unzips his leather jacket to reveal the top of a Transporter vest underneath. He sits down on one of the two couches that are facing each other across the room.

I pick up one of the remaining three bottles and tilt it back, taking one long swig. The soda stings the back of my throat causing me to hiccup. It tastes so good.

Rollins sits down on the couch across from Riley. He holds his bottle in one hand and drapes his free arm over the armrest, holding the half eaten Nutribar. Ria and I sit in the remaining seats on the couch next to my brother. Kingston stands a little further back by the bar that hovers over the two couches.

"I don't even know where to start," Riley says. He takes a long sip of his drink and finishes it off. "Your father's brilliant." He looks over at Kingston for a second before moving back to my brother. "Even though the vaccine he created was used for evil, he never intended it to be. What he created was magical. It changed the world."

A hard knock at the door pulls everyone's eyes away from the conversation.

"Who else knows you're here?" my brother questions in a low voice with clenched teeth. Rollins starts to get up off the couch. His eyes bounce around the room, not knowing where to hide.

"No one," Riley answers. His eyes dart from the door back to my brother. "This place was abandoned. I'm from your time. The only other person who knows I'm here is Dr. Dreadnought."

A knock sounds again, this time slightly louder.

"Citizens, you have to the count of ten to open this door in compliance of Statute 10036: harboring a known fugitive—or we will be forced to enter."

CHAPTER 31

OFF THE GRID

"Everyone to the back room," Riley whispers as he rushes across the small living room. "There's a false wall in the back that we can hide behind."

We enter the windowless room on the left and shove the bed over to the side. Riley places both hands on the wall and slides it over a few feet, revealing a small, dark opening that widens a couple of feet once inside.

Riley turns his body sideways and shimmies himself into the opening. As soon as Rollins follows him in, we hear an explosion go off in the living room. I picture a destroyed, splintered door scattered across the floor in a thousand pieces. All we can hear are heavy feet shuffling into the house.

Ria and I push our way in-between the two walls, moving as far down as possible.

Kingston, the last one to enter, slides the movable wall back into its original position, sealing out any light that might find its way in.

A single pair of footsteps enters the room. Afraid to exhale, I hold my breath. Ria grabs my hand and squeezes it tight.

"Clear," the loud, monotone voice says. I wait for the FootSoldier to exit, only to hear its boots trudge back to the center of the room. "The bed is askew in bedroom number two, General. It appears to have been pulled away from the wall."

Ria strengthens her grip around my hand. We're trapped. There's no other place to run. Why did we think we could trust this Riley Sanders guy? We don't know anything about him.

The FootSoldier marches forward, each step shaking the floor as it moves closer toward our hiding spot. I picture it holding out its mechanical hand and placing it on the thin makeshift wall on the other side of where we hide.

Vroom! Vroom!

The dune buggy's engine roars to life behind us in the garage.

"They're attempting to escape!" I hear a human's voice say through a radio on the other side of the wall. "All Soldiers report to the garage."

The drone doesn't move.

I picture it still standing on the other side of the wall. Its emotionless mind wants to investigate the room further, yet it's conflicted with the direct orders to retreat.

The FootSoldier finally gives up and plods out of the room to join the rest of the mini army.

The buggy revs its engine again, this time a little longer, as if it's about to take off on its own.

I hear the electronic garage door click and begin to open behind me.

Boom!

An explosion erupts behind us that rumbles the neighboring wall.

"What was that?" Ria's voice shakes.

"That was our ticket out of here," Riley announces confidently. He slides the false wall over a few feet again. Bright light immediately shoots in, illuminating the secret compartment. Riley holds up a little black box in the palm of his hand. His index finger still hovers over a little red button. "Well, we don't have a vehicle now, but it's probably best for us to stay off the streets anyway. Somehow they found out that you're here—that *we're* here."

Riley slides past us and grabs a full backpack out of the closest. "I had a feeling this wasn't gonna be easy."

No one makes the move to leave. Everyone is huddled up in the middle of the bedroom looking at Rollins for guidance.

Riley pauses to peer over at us before heading for the door. "They'll have reinforcements here any minute," he says. He slings the backpack over his shoulder. "And you don't want to be here when they arrive. Let's move."

We follow Riley out the front of the house, stepping over charred pieces of door and metal scattered across the front porch. The dune buggy now sits in the middle of the driveway and continues to burn. A thick trail of black smoke streams from the flaming wreckage. Pieces of scorched FootSoldier drones taken out by the blast lay sprinkled across the lawn.

"You did that?" my brother questions as he surveys the damage.

"It was the only way," Riley responds. "We needed a distraction." He tosses the little, black remote into the fire as we walk past the open garage.

"Where now?" Kingston asks. "You got another safe house around here for us to hide out in?"

Riley shakes his head. "No matter where we hide, they're gonna find us. It's time to get off the grid."

CHAPTER 32

OTHER ROOM

"How did you know the wall would protect us from the blast?" My brother asks Riley as he continues across the lawn at a slightly faster pace than everyone else. The backpack still hangs off one of his shoulders.

"I didn't," he responds. He glances over his shoulder. "Like I said, what other choice did we have?"

Rollins's eyes bore into Riley angrily. "But we could have been killed back there? How could you put us and the mission at risk like that?"

Riley stops and shakes his head in disbelief. "I don't need to explain myself again." He turns around to face the group. "I made an executive decision for our wellbeing. We all made it out alive. Now let me do my job."

With that, Riley ends the discussion and leads the way through what seems like an abandoned part of the neighborhood. We cut across an open, barren backyard that probably once belonged to a family before the war. The faces of my parents pop in my head. Did my mom know what my dad did for a living? Did she know that he's the reason Teles even exist…why her only two sons were kidnapped and forced to join a secret military army?

A ShadowHawk soars across the open, dark sky. Two more follow, flying side by side. The bright moonlight reflects off the menacing aerial drones as they approach the neighborhood.

"Everyone in here," Riley calls out. He rushes toward the back door of the closest house. A short overhang shadows the entryway, concealing us from view. No lights are on inside, but it doesn't mean the place is empty. Almost all of the houses we passed on this block don't seem to have power.

Without looking, Riley reaches over his shoulder and pulls a crowbar out of his pack. He wedges the end of the tool in-between the door and the frame to pry it open.

Two more Hawks race by overhead with only the blue flames of the engines lighting up the rear of the aircrafts.

"Think they're looking for us?" I ask as I watch the drones. They disappear over a hill, not far from where we stand.

"I think they're looking for whoever blew up that buggy and took out some of their Soldiers," Rollins answers as he observes Riley's attempts to get the door open.

"Come on, mate. It shouldn't take this long to get inside."

"It would help if I could see," Riley mutters loud enough for everyone to hear him. He grunts and puts all of his weight behind the force of the crowbar. A loud crack sounds through the darkness as the door finally creaks open.

"Everyone inside, but watch out," Riley whispers. He slides the crowbar back into his backpack and holds the door open for everyone to enter. "We don't know what's waiting for us in here."

I enter the house first, taking a cautious step into what resembles a kitchen. My eyes scan the pitch black room.

149

"It's too dark to see anything," I whisper. As soon as I turn my head, I spot a long, narrow shadow swing across the floor. Something hard strikes me in the stomach and knocks me back a few feet. I choke out a yelp.

Ria punches at the air and sends a wave of telekinetic force across the kitchen. A small body flings backward in the dark and smacks up against the wall on the opposite side of the room.

"Whoa! What was that?" Ria shrieks.

Riley turns on a flashlight and shines it across the room. The light finds a young, thin child sprawled out across the floor. The boy couldn't be any older than nine or ten years old. He has dark skin and short, tightly rolled dreadlocks springing in all different directions from the top of his head. Like everything else in Sol, his clothes are ragged and dirty.

The boy lifts himself halfway up and rubs at the side of his head. He rests his back against the wall behind him.

"What's your name, kid?" Riley inches closer to the boy. He holds the flashlight on the squinting boy's face. The child tries to use his hand to shield the bright light, but it's useless.

Ria moves around Riley and squats down next to the boy. "What's your name, sweetie? You know you almost scared us half to death sneaking up on us like that."

"You're the ones who broke into my house," the boy shouts. His eyes begin to water. "My momma's gonna be home any minute. You best leave before she gets here or she's gonna be upset."

"No she's not," Ria says, quickly calling the child's bluff. "You don't look like you've had a decent meal in weeks." Ria takes a Nutribar out of her pocket and hands it to the boy. "It's okay. You can trust us."

The boy refuses to look up but takes the food.

"My name's Jamarcus, but my mom used to call me Jam." He unwraps the Nutribar and takes a bite.

"Used to call you?" I lower the flashlight in Riley's hand, moving it off of the boy's face. "What happened to her?"

"Her name came up for registration, but mine didn't. She told me to stay here until she came back, but that was almost three weeks ago."

"And you've been here ever since?" Ria's voice sounds sincere. "All alone?"

A beam of red light shoots in through the back window and reflects off the wall just above Jam's head where he sits on the floor. I look through the kitchen window and spot several shadows in the backyard. A group of armed FootSoldiers moves across the lawn to approach the door. Their eyes glow a sinister red, reminding me again of my time spent at the Compound.

"We're about to have some company," I announce to the room. I squat down on the floor next to Ria. "Listen Jam, we're not bad people here, but we do have some pretty evil people after us. See those drones out there?" I move to the side so Jam can look out the window. The door stands slightly ajar since Riley pried it open.

Jam cranes his neck around me and nods his head.

"Do you think you can get rid of them? Tell them that you haven't seen anyone out here tonight?"

Riley turns off the flashlight. The room is now blanketed in darkness.

Jam continues to sit on the kitchen floor, unresponsive.

"We'll help you find your mom," I plead, as I grab the boy's arm. "As soon as we can get out of here."

151

Jam thinks about it for a second before responding. "You promise?"

I open my mouth to answer only to be interrupted by a bright red light beaming in through the back window, sending all of us—minus Jam—scurrying off into the next room.

The lead FootSoldier doesn't even knock. We peer around the corner and watch as a mini army of drones enters through the back door.

Jam picks a baseball bat off the ground and holds it tightly with both hands behind his head in a ready stance. "Stay back!"

The lead drone halts after taking a few steps into the kitchen.

"Citizen, we mean you no harm. Is there a parental unit currently at home?"

Jam shakes his head.

"We are looking for dangerous, rogue terrorists who have been identified in the area tonight. They wish to do harm to your Government." Five different headshots pop up across the drone's steel-armored chest. The glow from the images illuminates the small room. "A healthy reward will be given to you if you can inform us of their location."

Jam stands there, still gripping the bat. His eyes study the five pictures in front of him.

"All I want is my mom. Will you help me find her?" Jam pleads with the lead FootSoldier in a tiny voice.

The screen on the drone's chest disappears, returning to a sheet of black armor. "Of course we will." The FootSoldier's eyes continue to burn red, patiently waiting for the boy to tell them what they came for.

Jam lowers the bat and his eyes drop to the floor. With an apologetic facial expression he points in our direction. "They're in the other room."

CHAPTER 33

STRAY BULLET

As soon as the lead FootSoldier looks in our direction, Rollins extends his hand and shoots the heavy robot backward. The momentum of the flying Soldier knocks back the handful of other drones standing behind it in the doorway. Rollins flips his hand and slams the door closed on them.

"Come on!" Riley shouts. He darts toward the front door on the opposite side of the room. "We need to go."

Bullets erratically spray across the wall adjacent to the front door causing everyone to duck and take cover. I search the kitchen to locate the source of the gunfire. All I see are multiple pairs of red lights beaming back at me.

I spot my brother. He is standing in the middle of the living room, legs spread apart in a firm stance. His long shadow stretches across the floor as he holds out his arm, leveled at the group of tiny red beams of light.

"Come on, Rollins!" I shout over the loud firestorm coming from the other room.

"I'll catch up. Just get outside!" Rollins jumps to the side and dodges the shots.

A streak of moonlight shoots across the kitchen and into the living room. I catch a glimpse of Jam curled up on the floor on the other side of the door. He cups his tiny hands over both of his ears. His eyes are squeezed shut with a glimmer of tears running down both of his cheeks.

"We can't just leave him!" I shout. I turn halfway around to see the front door left wide-open. Riley, Ria, and Kingston have all managed to make it outside.

My brother grabs me by the arm and yanks me down. He pulls me around the corner of the couch as another round of bullets sprays across the living room.

"We don't even know how to defeat them," he says, as he tightens his grip on my arm. "I'm all for helping out the kid, but he's not worth getting killed over. Plus the little dude sold us out."

"Only because he wanted his mom," I say, halfway trying to convince myself, too.

Bang!

One of the FootSoldiers flies headfirst through the door that connects the kitchen with the living room. His steel body slams down onto the floor only a few feet in front of us. The immobile drone lays on its back in a freshly made indention in the middle of the floor. Sparks shoot up from just above its chest plate followed by a thin trail of smoke.

"What just happened?" I yell. I can't pull my eyes away from the now-lifeless FootSoldier that's within an arm's length of our crouching position on the floor. The eyes that previously glowed red now look like lifeless pieces of black coal. The artificial life that the drone was once given has now vanished.

"No clue, but whatever just happened saved us." Rollins reaches out to disarm the drone. "Heavier than I thought it would be." He grips the large gun with both hands. "They sure have come a long way in our time."

My brother pulls back on the slide before checking to see how many rounds remain in the magazine. He steps around the corner and fires the gun, blindly lighting up the remaining drones in the kitchen until the gun is out of ammunition.

He drops the heavy weapon at his feet.

Silence.

Rollins inches into the kitchen, alert and expecting another attack. I push myself up off the floor and follow him.

The place looks like a warzone. Bullet holes cover the majority of the walls and cabinets, along with the top of a table and set of overturned wooden chairs. Shell casings litter the floor.

Rollins walks over to the back door, or what's left of it, and glances out into the yard. He immediately finds Ria, Kingston, and Riley all hiding in the bushes. There's no sign of the other FootSoldiers that escaped.

"Looks like we're alone again," he announces, as he steps through the doorway.

I walk up to Jam and bend down to his side, gingerly shaking his arm. His hands still cover his ears as if he expects the attack to continue. He lies on his side with the front of his face buried in the floor, surrounded by small piles of shell casings.

"Hey, Jam, it's okay," I say, my voice rising on its own. "The bad drones are all gone. It's just us now."

Riley enters through the backdoor with his flashlight already turned on. He shines the light on the frightened kid's face. Ria bends down and runs her hand soothingly over his head.

"It's okay, sweetie. There's nothing to be afraid of now."

A grave look washes over Ria's face. She places two fingers to the side of his neck and holds them there for a few seconds, before biting down on her bottom lip with a grimace.

"Nic." She glances up to make eye contact with me. "I'm not getting a pulse. I think a stray bullet got him." She rolls Jam's body over onto his back and I notice a tiny red hole in the middle of his chest. A trail of blood runs down his shirt. Ria turns her head and holds her ear down to his chest. She closes her eyes and shakes her head.

"At least he's with his mom now," Kingston says as he walks up to where Ria and I kneel down next to Jam's body. "He's gotta be in a better place—"

A round of bullets fires in through the open back door.

I turn my attention to the backyard. My mind is consumed with hatred—sick and tired of all the pointless killing. Pairs of red lights bounce around in the darkness, ready for a second attack.

Rollins grabs me by the back of the shirt, again, and yanks me out of the line of fire. "Come on, we can't stay here!"

My brother latches onto me, dragging me after him toward the front door. Everyone else scrambles to follow.

"What now?" Ria says as we make it outside and cut over onto another dark street.

Everyone turns to Riley expecting an answer.

"We need to find somewhere to stay for the night," he says. "There's only one place I know that will take us in. Pray there's room for all of us."

CHAPTER 34

A FRIEND OF A FRIEND

We travel on foot to the outskirts of another dilapidated neighborhood on the opposite side of Sol's main road. Like the majority of Jam's neighborhood, there are no lights on in any of the houses we pass. Frustratingly, Riley avoids telling us anything about the mission until we get to wherever he is taking us. He has warned us about sector spies that search for traitors who do not follow the Government's laws. Somehow we are supposed to trust this complete stranger that has a knack for putting us in situations that don't end up in our favor.

"I think this is the place," Riley says uncertainly. We stand in front of another single-story house with a small garage attached to the side, similar to the last safe house we were in. "Dr. Dreadnought told me this place is our fallback. There's a family inside willing to help us hide out for the night, but they don't know anything about the Transporter or the mission, so keep all of that quiet."

Riley raps at the door three solid times, then steps back to join us.

"Yes?" a deep, male voice answers. The door remains closed, along with the curtains on either side of the entrance.

"A friend of a friend sent us," Riley calmly answers. He confidently turns to the side and eyes my brother.

"I sure hope you're right about this place," Rollins spits out between clenched teeth.

The door creaks open allowing only a small cone of light to sneak onto the front porch.

"Were you followed?" The person keeps his face hidden in the shadows.

"I don't think so," Riley answers. His voice shakes as he turns and glances back over his shoulder. The empty street behind us remains quiet.

"You're safe here, my friends," the mysterious, deep voice says. The door opens up a little wider, inviting us in. The man holds a flashlight to his side, illuminating only the tiled-floor he stands on. He keeps his other hand on the door handle ready to close it as soon as everyone enters.

Inside, everything is dark. The only source of light is what's coming from the flashlight, as the man scurries around us to move to the front of the group. The beam of light dances around the floor in a rhythmic pattern matching the man's stride, all while keeping the man's face and true identity hidden in the shadows.

"You can call me Moses." The old man raises the flashlight and waves it across our faces. "Listen up. I only have two rules. One: Keep to yourself. Don't talk to anyone else in the house but the people currently in this room. And two," he pauses to sweep the beam across our faces again, "you have to be out of here before dawn. I can't risk anyone seeing you leave in the daylight."

Riley nods his head. "Yes, sir. We understand."

Moses then leads us down a short hallway in a single-file line, passing rooms on both sides. The first room we pass is the only one in the hall that has a light on.

As we pass the door, a young boy with dark hair and hollow eyes pokes his head out.

"New arrivals?" the young boy asks with a low voice.

Everyone turns to look at the boy, but Moses is the only one to respond.

"Go back to bed and mind your business." The man shifts his attention back to us. "That's my grandson, Portland. He lives here with his father. Don't mind him." He nods his head to end the short statement.

We continue down the hall until we reach the last room. Moses opens the door to a small room with four single beds, each one occupying its own wall. "Two of you will have to share a bed. All of the other rooms are full. If you're hungry, it's too late. The kitchen's closed." Moses pauses to sweep the light across our faces again. "If you get up early enough, we'll feed you in the morning before sending you on your way."

"My brother and I will share a bed. No problem. Thank you, sir. You don't wanna know what we've been through tonight."

Moses studies my brother's face before giving him another sharp nod. "Don't need the details, kid, just get some rest." He hands Riley the flashlight in his hand. "It's not safe for you to have this on for too much longer, but it will at least help you all get settled. I'm assuming you understand the risk I'm taking here, right?" The man pauses to wait for a response.

Riley nods his head. He turns to walk the old man to the door and hands him something, briefly shaking the man's hand. They exchange a couple of mumbled words before Moses closes the bedroom door.

"Everything okay?" Rollins questions. He stands with the rest of the group in the middle of the room.

"Yea, I had to pay the old man off," Riley says, like he does this sort of thing all the time. "Some of these places will turn you in for the reward if you don't pay enough to keep them quiet."

So much for human kindness.

Kingston is the first to break away from the group, choosing the bed closest to the door. He sits down in the middle and slides his hand across the thin sheet. "So, what's our next move?" He begins to unlace and take off his boots.

"I'm sure everyone saw the billboard earlier on the way in," Riley begins, as he removes the backpack from his shoulders and places it down on the ground next to one of the beds. He slides the bag partially underneath the bed.

I nod. "Yea, he was giving some kind of speech in a video. Is he a teacher?"

"Not exactly. Your father, Dr. McCready, doesn't work for the Government in this particular time period. I believe that's the reason Dr. Dreadnought picked this year to send you back to."

Rollins sits down on an empty bed and leans forward. He rests his elbows on his thighs. "That's right, I remember him saying something about how he used to work for a private company before the Government bought it out, right?"

Riley nods his head and points the flashlight onto the floor in the center of the room. "Tomorrow night, your father is giving a talk at the Sol Lecture Hall to some of the top scientists in the sector." Riley focuses on my brother. "While working on a new vaccine, he stumbled upon a mutation in the genetic code that creates the ability to levitate. At this point, your father probably doesn't even know what he has. But once the Government finds out about it, they'll force him to turn over the formula so they can mass produce it. They'll offer him a high level Government job, paying him whatever he wants, thus, starting up the Tele program as we know—"

161

A light, single knock at the door causes Riley to freeze. Everyone's eyes dart in the direction of the sound.

"Moses?" Riley's voice calls to dead air.

Nothing.

Kingston gets up and opens the door. The sound of another door closing echoes down the hall.

"No one's here." He shakes his head and closes the bedroom door again.

"Dr. Dreadnought provided us with passes to get into the lecture," Riley lowers his voice, before leaning forward, almost whispering, "but I don't know how safe it'll be. The Government's Army will be searching for us, maybe even expect us to show up. I think the safest thing is to split up, maybe even enter at different times."

"We have all afternoon to figure out the logistics," Rollins says in the middle of a wide yawn. "What we really need is a good night sleep. Let's take turns keeping watch. I'll go—"

"I'll go first," I say, drowning out my brother's tired voice. "Everyone else get some rest. I'm good for at least an hour or two."

Riley turns off the flashlight, cloaking the room in complete darkness.

I lay still for a couple of minutes and stare at what I imagine is the wall across the room. Staying awake might prove to be a little more difficult than I originally thought.

CHAPTER 35

RUDE AWAKENING

I wake suddenly, my eyes focusing on a blurry shadow across the room. A young man, possibly in his early twenties, with short, dark hair squats down by the head of Riley's bed. His back faces me and I can see his head move slightly as he examines whatever's in front of him. He has a long, deep scar that runs down the back of his shaved head and disappears under his shirt collar.

"Hey!" I yell, causing the man to jump. "What're you doing in here?"

The man jumps and drops the bag in his hands. He spins around to find me sitting halfway up in my bed looking befuddled. He has something small concealed in the palm of his hand. He stands up and stuffs the object deep down into his pocket.

Rollins stirs next to me and lifts his head. "What's going on?" he says in a slight panic. "What time is it?" He rolls over, now facing the man.

"You should have paid Moses more," the man mumbles at us, before quickly making his way for the door. "He's the one who gave you up to the authorities, not me."

Rollins jumps up and scrambles after the man as he flees the room.

"What's going on?" Kingston groggily watches Rollins duck out the door. He rubs his eyes as he tries to make sense of the commotion.

Riley finally wakes up and glances down at his open backpack on the floor next to his bed. He jerks the bag off the floor and begins rifling through it.

Ria sits up. "Is something wrong? Everything there?"

Rollins darts back into the room out of breath and slams the door shut behind him. "We have company outside. We gotta go!"

"But that little thief stole our lecture passes!" Riley shouts as the door crashes open.

A half dozen uniformed men push their way inside the tiny room. Their guns are already drawn, waving threateningly in our faces as they scream for us to freeze. All of the men are wearing bulletproof vests that read: GA POLICE across the front. One officer grabs my brother and shoves him up against the wall. He tries to resist, but he flips his gun around and launches the butt end of the weapon into Rollins's midsection.

My brother collapses to the floor.

"Everyone on your feet!" the lead officer yells, ordering everyone off their beds. "Hands up. You're all under arrest for suspicion of terrorism!"

Riley exhales and drops the bag. He raises his arms over his head. The rest of us follow suit.

Rollins pushes himself up off the floor, holding a hand gingerly across his stomach.

"Fine, we'll do what you say."

164

CHAPTER 36

MANKIND

As we are shuffled single-file down the hall at gunpoint, I see an old man whom I can only assume is Moses since I never clearly saw his face the night before. His long, thin arms are casually folded across his flannel shirt that's tucked into his jeans. He has a full head of light red hair and a thick beard covering the majority of his face. He looks like a farmer. The tall, skinny young man I discovered moments earlier in our room stands next to him. He has dark, hollow eyes and a sunken face. Both men wear looks of contempt, obviously not the least bit guilty for turning us in.

"Thanks for contacting us," the officer to my rear says to Moses. He wears Riley's backpack slung over one shoulder. "The Government applauds you for your honor and commitment." He shakes the old man's hand and places something into his palm that Moses pockets. He winks at Moses as he passes, before exiting the front door.

"I'll give you a call if any more show up," Moses says. "Thanks officers."

We are led down to a large military truck painted in desert camouflage. One of the soldiers unlatches and opens two steel doors in the back, before pulling down a small stepladder. He tosses Riley's bag into the back up the truck.

"Up you go," the soldier orders. He shoves the tip of his gun into Riley's back. "One at a time, watch your step."

Once everyone has climbed in, we sit down on the benches that line the walls of the inside of the truck. Two guards follow us up the ladder and close the doors behind them. I hear a padlock click shut outside, followed by a double knock. Each officer moves down the line and handcuffs our wrists, then sits down at the end of the bench closest to the doors.

"The prisoners are secure." The officer next to me radios the front cab. "Let's get back to base. It's not getting any cooler back here."

"10-4," the handheld radio hisses back.

As soon as the truck shifts into gear and starts moving, I notice the temperature has indeed risen. It crosses my mind that this could be some sort of torture device, but the officers look just as uncomfortable as we are.

I glance across the aisle at Rollins. He bites at his bottom lip, while his eyes focus on the officer sitting next to me. I glance over at the man. The first thing I see is the large gun strapped to his back. Each time the truck hits a bump, the barrel end of his gun scrapes against the wall behind it, making a rattling sound. A handgun is holstered on his waist, along with various other strange weapons and tools I've never seen before.

"So what did you do?" the officer next to Rollins says to me. "Plot an assassination attempt on the President?"

"You know we're not supposed to talk to the prisoners," the guard next to me spits back. He glares at the other officer to prove his seriousness. After a brief moment of silence, he turns his attention back down to his boots.

"What's the harm?" the first officer asks. He wipes away a stream of sweat from his forehead. He scrunches his eyebrows and scowls at the man across from him. He leans forward. "Come on kid, what did you do?" He stares at me and waits for a response.

I grit my teeth as my eyes dart over to my brother. *What do I say?*

The truck swerves and hits a deep pothole in the road. The officer across the aisle falls forward, but catches himself on his partner's leg.

I reach my hand out to disarm the startled, fallen officer. His pistol unholsters itself and flies straight into my open hand. I grip the gun using both cuffed hands.

"Don't move!"

The officer next to me pushes his partner off of him and reaches for his gun. The truck continues to drive down the bumpy road, jostling us up and down.

"Drop it!" I extend my arms out a little more to move the tip of the gun closer to his face.

He releases his hand from his holster, before raising both arms in the air. The officer on the floor cautiously pushes himself up and slowly raises his hands as well.

"You kids are already in enough trouble. You sure you want to add kidnapping Government officers to the list?"

"Keys," Rollins demands. He holds his cuffed hands out to the officer next to him.

The man's eyes shift to mine before shaking his head in disapproval. He reaches for the key ring on his belt and then unlocks us one at a time.

"You know you're not going to get away with this?" The officer who was on the ground is now sitting on a bench. He stares up at Kingston. Kingston ignores him and cuffs the man's hands together, locking them around a small pole that runs below the benches. Ria does the same to the other officer on the opposite bench. Then, together, they gather up the remaining weapons that were on the two men and hand the smaller items to Riley who puts them into the backpack.

"We have to sir," I say with honesty, answering the man after no one else does. "Mankind depends on it."

The officer scoffs at my statement, turning his face to the side.

"You're crazy," the other man mutters, echoing his partner's snide tone.

We huddle in front of the rear doors.

"What now?" Kingston asks. He holds one of the large guns close to his chest. Rollins holds the other one, while Riley and Ria both have handguns.

Everyone's eyes land on me.

"Why's everyone looking at me?" I say with surprise. "I don't have plan."

"I have an idea," Ria says, raising her voice. "Stand back."

She raises both of her fists into a fighter's stance, then punches several times in the air and releases a powerful, sweeping telekinetic wave at the door.

Bam!

The doors bend outward, but the lock outside holds them in place.

Ria turns to the side and releases a jump kick in the air, followed by another barrage of punches. The two doors buckle even farther, before a powerful thrust finally snaps the lock. The doors fly open and crash into the sides of the truck.

The driver slams on the brakes and sends everyone, except the two officers, sliding back toward the front of the truck.

"Come on!" I stand the closest to the exit and leap out of the back of the truck. The bright sunlight blinds me as soon as my feet make contact with the asphalt. One at a time, everyone else jumps out.

The man in the parked car behind us blows his horn and shakes an angry fist out the window. He yells something, but it's lost in the chaos around us.

I point the raised gun in my hand toward the front of his car. The driver quickly throws his hands up in the air. More cars come to a stop behind him, clogging up the busy street.

"Where can we go?" Ria says. She searches my face for an answer. "We've gotta move."

"This way," I say, pointing across the road. "This may be our only chance."

They begin to follow me to a narrow alley forming a path between two rundown buildings.

I poke my head around the corner of the vehicle, only to recoil quickly as gunfire erupts from the front half of the truck.

"Well, maybe not."

CHAPTER 37

HIT

An internal steel door connecting the rear of the truck with the front cab opens. An officer slowly slides his gun out through the opening and lines up his shot.

"Look out!" Kingston ducks, shoving me and Ria out of the way just as the soldier pulls the trigger. Kingston props up his gun on the floor of the truck.

"They're coming through the inside door!" He squeezes the trigger and fires off several rounds into the rear of the cab. Bullets ricochet off the back door and wall, cutting off the attacker.

"We need to get out of here!" Rollins shouts. He aimlessly shoots his gun toward the front of the truck. "We have to find somewhere to take—"

Bullets fly at us from above, punching holes into the side of the military vehicle.

Rollins searches the building across the road. He points toward an open window a few floors up. "Sniper! Everyone get underneath the truck!"

Another round of bullets strikes the side of the truck as we scamper underneath the vehicle.

"What are we gonna do?" I scream. "They're everywhere!"

An out of control, skidding car slams into the side of another vehicle parked between the building and our truck. The sound of glass shattering drowns out the gunfire for a split second, followed by a woman's shrill scream. The driver jumps out of her car, only to be immediately struck by an oncoming vehicle speeding through the warzone. The woman bounces off the front end of the vehicle and is catapulted at least fifteen feet through the air. Her body lands in an awkward position, her neck broken.

Kingston stares blankly out into the road. His eyes are locked on the unconscious woman's face, unable to look away.

"Hey, are you okay?" Rollins says. He army crawls over to Kingston and grabs him by the arm.

"Ahh, what?" Kingston responds. He shakes his head to the side. "Yeah, mate. I'm okay."

"Doesn't it seem like they've moved back a little? They're set up behind those lined up cars." Rollins points across the street where groups of armed soldiers are huddled behind barriers.

"With reinforcements," Kingston adds. He studies the army of men across the street.

"Somehow we need to get to the other side of that barricade without being noticed." Rollins says.

"Without being noticed?" Riley jumps in. "What about the manhole? Where do you think it leads?" He nods over to the circular sewage lid directly behind the front left tire of the truck.

"Aren't you the one who's supposed to have all the answers?" I shout. My eyes shoot daggers in Riley's direction. "Didn't Dreadnought prep you for a situation like this?" I grab the front of Riley's shirt. "I think Kingston was right. Maybe you are working with the Government. GAs sure seem to keep popping up everywhere we go since you managed to *find* us in the middle of the desert." I take a deep breath before adding, "And you sure knew an awful lot about fugitive rewards!"

"It's not his fault," Ria yells. She tears my hand away from his shirt. "He didn't know Moses was a traitor."

Rollins slides over and grunts. The large gun in his hands digs into his upper chest, making an indention in his shirt. "Will all of you just quit arguing and figure out how to get that lid up? We're gonna run out of ammo before they do, and I don't wanna be here to find out what happens when we do." With that, he fires off another round at the soldiers across the street.

"Come on," Ria says. "I'm need your help if we're gonna move this thing."

I nod my head. Together we aim our palms toward the closed manhole cover. I can feel the lid beginning to rise when another military truck races up and smashes into the back of an already abandoned car in the middle of the road. It comes to a stop parallel to the back of our truck.

"Where did they go?" a voice screams behind us. Multiple pairs of boots exit the back of the truck.

Ria and I slide the manhole cover off to the side.

"Under the truck," a deep, booming voice orders. "Don't let them escape!"

"Let's move, people," Rollins orders. "Riley, you first, then Nic and Ria. Make sure it's safe down there. Kingston and I will hold them off up here as long as we can." He ends the sentence by sweeping his gun across the ground, erratically firing at the street. A barrage of screams from a group of spectators follows.

"Rollins," I say, as I grab his arm. I open my mouth, but no words come out. The look on my face tells him exactly what I'm thinking.

"I'm right behind you, little bro. Trust me."

I watch as Riley squeezes himself into the hole, followed by Ria and then me.

I climb down a steel ladder, one rung at a time, allowing the darkness to swallow me whole. I'm only a few feet down before I lose sight of the ladder in front of me.

"Anyone reach the bottom yet?" I shout over the loud gunfire thundering above me.

"Yeah," Riley calls. He turns on his flashlight and swings it around. I can see the beam of golden light cut through the darkness and bounce off the walls of the narrow opening. "It looks like this tunnel goes in both directions." He shines the flashlight up the ladder.

"Come on guys!" I tilt my head up toward the street. I wonder if they can even hear me.

The only response I receive from above is more violent gunfire.

"Watch out!" I hear Kingston shout during a short pause in action. A hollow, clanking sound follows, like a large gun being dropped onto the asphalt.

"Ahhh!" Rollins howls. "I've been hit!"

CHAPTER 38

INTO THE DARKNESS

Rollins's face appears in the opening above me. His eyes find me more than halfway down the ladder. He tries to say something, but his face can only form a grimace.

Kingston comes into view. "I'm gonna help him onto the ladder, but you need to get him the rest of the way down. He won't be able to climb down on his own."

More gunfire causes Kingston to duck out of the way. He picks up the gun at his side and fires back across the street. His face tenses up as he squeezes the trigger, the light from the gun highlighting the tattoo on his chin.

"Kingston!"

Kingston drops the gun and uses both hands to help my brother onto the ladder. He can only manage to hold onto the rungs with one hand at the top, his injured arm hanging freely.

I hold one hand out above me. "Let go, Rollins! I have you."

My brother's limp body falls backward as he releases himself from the ladder with a loud grunt. Using my power, I guide him down the rest of the way to the floor like a floating ghost.

Once he's safe, Kingston and I finish the descent and join the rest of the group at the bottom.

"It's crazy up there." Kingston grabs the gun strapped to his shoulder. He checks to see how many bullets are left in the magazine. "They've got the place completely surrounded and we're almost out of ammo. The other gun's out and this magazine's practically empty."

The gunfire above us ceases, pulling everyone's eyes to the ceiling. A low whistle replaces the sound, quickly crescendoing in volume.

"What is that?" Ria questions. Like everyone else, her gaze is fixed on the hole in the ceiling.

Boom!

"Watch out!" I tackle my brother out of the way.

A bright light rips through the center of the vehicle and levitates the battered military truck at least ten feet into the air. A blaze of fire shoots down through the open manhole, illuminating our surroundings for a few seconds before the truck comes crashing back down onto the street.

Rollins releases a deep moan and rolls onto his back. He tries to push me off of him, but he doesn't have the strength. The fire dissipates, leaving the underground room unharmed.

"Good Lord, what was that?" Riley says.

Everyone lays scattered across the floor.

"I think they just dropped a bomb on us," Kingston coughs. "Anyone hurt?"

175

Riley shines his flashlight around the room, confirming everyone is okay.

"Before we do anything else, we need to get that bullet out of your arm," Riley says to my brother as he sits up. He directs the light onto the injured arm from across the room. "I think I have a first aid kit in here, or at least something to slow down the bleeding." He begins digging through his backpack.

Muffled voices shout from above. My ears are still ringing from the blast. I can't make out exactly what they are saying, but I know they're not here to help us.

"Everyone move!" Kingston yells. He lifts his gun and fires a couple of shots toward the hole in the ceiling, pushing the officers back.

I help Rollins off the ground and together we stumble across the room to join everyone else inside an adjacent tunnel. A large pipe shields us from view. I gently lay my brother down on the ground and prop his back up against the curved, metal wall.

"What should we do?" I say, out of breath.

"They're just going to send reinforcements down all of the other entryways," Riley says flatly. He shines the flashlight on the walls around us. "We have to find a way out of here."

"And we can't go back up," Rollins adds in a frustrated voice. He rotates his shoulder blade, causing his face to tighten up in anguish.

Riley pulls an extra shirt out of his bag and hands it to me. "Tie this around the wound. It'll have to do until—"

Something behind us moves in the dark and causes a tiny splash a few feet away.

Everyone turns toward the sound. Riley stretches the light down the tunnel, scanning every surface.

"What was that?" Ria whispers. "GAs? FootSoldiers?"

Riley sweeps the light further down and searches for the cause of the sound. "Maybe a rat? Could've been anything."

"Riley, move the light over there," Rollins orders. He points in the direction the noise seemed to come from. "Doesn't it look like it opens up over there a little?"

We hear another light splash, as if whoever, or whatever, is making the noise is trying to scare us away.

"I think I see something," Riley shouts. He jumps into the darkness. The beam from his flashlight turns the corner and darts down the tunnel where Rollins was just pointing. Heavy footsteps splash through the shallow water as he runs, slowly fading, until we can't hear him anymore.

"Anything?" I call out hopefully.

"Help me up, Nic!" Rollins says. His hand grabs at my arm. "Someone needs to go after him."

"It certainly isn't going to be you," I command, though I pull him up to my side anyways. He leans back on the wall behind him.

"AHHH!" Riley answers with a throat-curdling scream that reverberates off the metal walls.

"Riley?" Kingston shouts. "Are you okay? What's going on down there?"

No response.

"Rollins is right," Ria whispers. "Someone needs to go after him."

"Nic," Kingston slaps me on the arm. "That's our cue. Let's go check it out. Ria, you stay here with Rollins."

Silently I agree, knowing I have no choice.

Kingston and I blindly creep down the tunnel, following the faint glow of Riley's flashlight that remains on but no longer moves. The only sounds I hear are our boots making tiny splashes with each step.

"I don't think it's the Government's Army," Kingston whispers. He holds his hand out to stop me from entering the side tunnel. "If it was, I think they would have attacked by now."

I nod my head even though I know he cannot see me.

"You hear that?" Kingston whispers. He reaches out and grabs my forearm.

Riley's flashlight clicks off.

"Come any closer and your friend dies."

CHAPTER 39

FALLING

When the light clicks back on, we see Riley sitting down on the ground before us. A young, thin boy with dark skin and a shaved head hovers behind him holding a large knife just under Riley's chin.

"Hold up, mate," Kingston says as he raises his hands. "We just came to get our friend. We don't want any trouble."

The boy flips the bright light over with one hand and shines it back onto our faces.

"Who are you? What're you doing down here?" His voice sounds little, yet shrill.

I steal a quick glimpse over at Kingston.

"We don't want any trouble," I repeat. I hold up my hand to shield the light. Trails of yellow pop up behind him from the opposite end of the dark tunnel.

The boy begins to turn to investigate, but only for a second, before his eyes shift back to us.

Riley doesn't flinch. The boy pulls Riley's head closer to his chest and repositions the knife against his bare neck.

"Friends of yours?" Kingston questions. His voice cracks midsentence betraying his nerves. He imitates me by partially shielding the bright light with his hand.

Before the boy can respond, we hear a deep voice say, "I think I see something up ahead!" Beams of light bounce off the walls and floor.

"GAs," the young boy mutters to himself, like it's an everyday occurrence. He shoves Riley forward onto the ground and vanishes into the darkness behind him, stealing our only flashlight.

"Where did he go?" I yell. "He was just here!" I blindly search the wall, looking for any trace of an exit. It's impossible to see anything in the dark, other than the growing beams of light rushing toward us.

"Come on," Kingston shouts. "We don't have time for the kid." He grabs my forearm to let me know he's close. "We need to get back and warn your brother and Ria."

The three of us dart down the tunnel, clumsily bumping into each other as we move. As soon as I turn the corner, I collide with both Ria and Rollins. I fall hard to the ground, hitting my forehead on the wall.

"I thought you two were gonna stay back?" I blink my eyes as I search for their invisible faces in the darkness.

Ria responds with a low groan.

"Still have a hard head, I see," Rollins says jokingly.

"They're right behind us," Riley screams, as he rushes up and drags me to my feet. "GAs!" He pulls a lighter out of his pocket and ignites a small flame.

"And a little boy," I add, out of breath. I hold my palm across my forehead and massage it. The flame dances back and forth as Riley moves around the tunnel. "But he disappeared before we could follow him."

"I think I found another opening back there right before he snuck up behind me," Riley says, his voice laced with panic. He pulls the flickering flame a little closer to his face and raises his eyebrows. "Could be a place to hide, if anything?"

I glance back down the tunnel behind us and spot the flashlights moving closer, becoming larger. I bite my bottom lip. "Rollins, are you okay? Can you move?" I wrap my arm around him and allow him to put all of his weight on me.

He nods his head. "Doesn't seem like I have much of a choice, now do I?" He releases a chuckle, followed by another moan. "Come on."

One at a time, we follow Riley, entering the smaller side tunnel behind us.

"I think I saw the kid somewhere over here," he whispers. "Wait, over here!" He holds the portable flame close to one of the walls and begins pushing on it using his one free hand. The low, rounding wall begins to shift and form the shape of a hidden door.

"Unreal!" Kingston gasps. He steps forward to help Riley. The wall slides inward a few feet, as it scrapes against the hard floor underneath.

"I know I saw something up there," a loud, deep voice shouts behind us in the dark. The tiny trails of light continue to grow, streaking the dark, seemingly endless tunnel.

"Everyone inside," Riley whispers.

Once everyone's in, we slide the door back into place and stand as still as possible. I hear multiple people rush past us through the shallow water, not trying to hide their presence at all.

181

Riley strikes the lighter in his hand again and produces another dancing flame. He pivots around, waving it out in front of him.

"Where are we?" Ria whispers. "What is this place?"

"Doesn't seem like it goes back too far." I place a hand on the wall next to me. It's cold to the touch, a completely different material than the ones that make up the other tunnels outside.

"Hanging in there, Rollins?" Ria whispers. Her voice makes me look at my brother. He rests most of his weight against me, yet he's slouched over in pain.

He shakes his head in the dim glow of the flame and releases another moan. His sweat-covered face has grown a shade paler, while his eyelids are starting to droop down a bit. The normal spark in his eyes has vanished. He looks like he has aged at least twenty years in the past ten minutes.

"We need to get that thing out of you." I readjust my arm around his shoulders. "We're running out of time. This tunnel has to lead to somewhere."

We shuffle a couple of steps forward and the wall hooks sharply to the right. I take my first step around the corner and my boot suddenly doesn't find solid footing underneath.

I stumble and fall forward into the hole, releasing Rollins from my grip as I let out a scream. I overcorrect myself as I fall and my head strikes the ledge behind me, instantly knocking me out.

CHAPTER 40

T

A loud, muffled scream jolts me awake.

My vision is blurred as I look around. *Where am I?*

I lay in a small bed in an equally small, windowless room that is not well lit. The four rounded walls are one color—dark gray, adding extra shadows to the room. Other than the bed, the room is empty. The bedding is made of torn out pages from old books and newspapers, resting on top of a paper thin mattress. My eyes focus on a date printed across the top of a paper from almost thirty years ago. As I sit up, the bed rustles as a few of the pieces of paper fall to the ground.

A low groaning voice begs for help from another room.

I jump to my feet and immediately have to lie back down. The back of my head throbs in pain making me feel dizzy and nauseous. The last thing I remember is falling headfirst into a dark hole.

Another groan erupts outside my room.

"Yes! I can feel it!" An irritated voice says, followed by a crash to the ground.

I push myself out of bed again to investigate. I still wear the Transporter vest, along with my T-shirt and pants, but my boots are missing.

Lying in a bed in the next room over is my brother. Ria, Kingston, and Riley all crowd around him. A man sits bent over in a swivel chair opposite them, retrieving surgical tools off the ground and placing them onto a wooden table by his side. He wears a red bandana over his mouth with a small headlamp attached to his forehead. Long dreadlocks hang down the man's back, loosely tied up just above his waist. Every time he faces my brother, he illuminates his blood-soaked arm with the bright spotlight.

"You have to keep him still," the man orders, sounding aggravated. He holds an extra long pair of tweezers in his hand. The tips of the utensil are coated in dark red. "Hold down both of his arms and legs. Secure him."

I clear my throat as I stand in the open doorway.

Everyone turns around but the man, who continues to work on Rollins. My brother's eyes roll over to me.

"Hey, you're awake!" Ria says with surprise. She leaves Rollins's bedside to join me in the doorway.

"Is he gonna be okay?" I ask. I place an arm around her and she kisses me on the lips.

"If my daughter, Theresa, hadn't found you all when he did," the man says, "we might be removing his arm as we speak. But if he can just sit still, I think we can save it."

Daughter?

"Try getting operated on without anesthesia," Rollins hisses through his clenched teeth. His face is ashen. Both of his hands grab

184

at the sides of the bed. His fingernails dig into edge of the thin mattress.

I bite my bottom lip and forget about my headache for a second.

"Where are we?" I question as I examine the new room. It's identical to the one I woke up in, other than the small wooden bedside table and all of the people crowded around it.

"Theresa and her family live here," Ria says. "We're just in a different area of the sewer."

"T!" a girl's frustrated voice says behind me. "Call me T!"

"Your God-given name is Theresa," the older man barks back. His eyes do not leave my brother's arm. "She wants me to call her T, like she's some kind of thug," the man mutters to himself and the rest of the room.

The young girl, Theresa—T, slides herself by me through the doorway. I can see why we originally thought she was a boy back in the tunnel based on her shaved head. She wears a tattered white shirt and jeans that are both full of small holes and tears, darkened from dirt and overuse.

"You're lucky I found you when I did," the girl mutters. She moves close to her father's side and peers over his shoulder, as if she's grading him on the procedure. "My father was once one of the best veterinarians in Sol before the Uprising. They tried to recruit him to be a surgeon for the GA, but he turned them down."

"That's enough," Theresa's father sharply cuts her off. The extracted bullet drops from his grasp and clinks on the floor. "We don't need to tell them all of our business. Go grab me a rag and a bowl of water from the other room."

I glance at my brother's arm. The area around the wound is covered in a dark purple halo. His bloody shirt has been removed, along with the Transporter vest.

185

"Where's Rollins's vest?" I ask in a panic, turning toward Ria.

"In the pack," Riley answers from across the room. He still wears the bag slung over one shoulder.

"Maybe I should hold onto it," I suggest to Riley, but he either doesn't hear me or simply ignores me. All of his attention is focused on my brother in front of him.

"Okay, I need you kids to hold him down again. Time to clean out the wound."

Ria and I move to the opposite side of the bed. I take one of his legs and press down on his thigh and ankle; while Ria joins Riley and Kingston to help secure his other leg, arms, and torso.

Theresa returns with a bowl and rag in her hands. She places them down on the nightstand next to an unrolled piece of thick cloth filled with surgical tools.

Theresa's father dips the rag into the bowl of water and presses it against the open wound that continues to drain blood. He firmly holds the rag there as Rollins thrashes around in the bed, choking back a scream.

"Theresa, I need you to press down here," her father says. He places her hand over the center of the rag. "Whatever you do, don't let up."

The man begins to thread a needle quickly, holding the eye up in the light. When he's done, he lifts the rag slightly off my brother's arm. The bleeding seems to have slowed a little bit.

"I'm not gonna lie," the man says. "This is going to hurt." He digs the needle into Rollin's upper arm and begins to stitch up the wound. My brother grits his teeth and squeezes his eyes shut.

The job takes a long couple of minutes to complete.

Rollins breathes a sigh of relief once it's finally done. Sweat drenches his entire face.

"I can't move my arm, Doc." My brother turns to face the older man.

"That's expected. You really shouldn't do anything for the next few days except rest. Let the wound heal." He lowers the bandana from his face and allows it to hang around his neck. He then begins to gather up all of his tools, wrapping the thick piece of cloth around them. "I couldn't tell you how valuable this equipment is. It's saved us numerous times since we've been down here."

"How long have you been living down here?" I ask as I study the doctor's face for the first time.

"Theresa, will you take these into the other room and sterilize them for me?" The doctor hands his daughter the cloth-lined surgical kit using both hands. He turns his attention back to me. "Maybe a year or two, possibly three? We don't really keep track of dates down here too well, especially without any windows to see daylight. When her mother and older brother were called to register, they never returned. I, of course, looked into it, but no one could provide me with any answers of their whereabouts."

"So you took matters into your own hands," I say. My eyes find my brother again.

The doctor's stare wanders off, burning a hole through the wall across the room. He shakes his head. "You do what you have to do to survive."

A loud bang interrupts the brief moment of silence. Theresa rushes back into the room. Her hands are stained a dark red from cleaning the surgical tools.

"We have company upstairs, Daddy."

CHAPTER 41

BECAUSE OF US

"Are these the same guys causing all the commotion earlier?" Theresa's father stares at a monitor they have hooked up to film a live feed of the entrance door.

"Yeah, they're here for us. They—" I say, before being waved off by the man.

"We don't need to know all of your business either. The less we know the better."

"Is there another way out of here?" Rollins asks, trudging into the room. "You must know all of these tunnels after being down here for so many years." Riley hands Rollins his Transporter vest and he puts it on.

"We've gotta reach the lecture hall," Ria adds. She grabs my hand. "We can't even begin to explain how important it is."

The monitor shows at least ten officers huddled around the hidden entrance, each holding a gun with a flashlight attached to it. One soldier holds up a long, thick pole at his side that is almost as tall as he is. With the assistance of another man, the two of them pick up the pole and begin to ram it into the side of the wall. The sound of the pounding rumbles all the way down to where we stand in the small room.

"You have to leave now," Theresa's father says. His eyes shift back and forth. "But your friend here really should be resting." He shakes his head, unable to make the decision.

The determined men above us continue to ram the wall.

"Please, sir," Ria says. She lets go of my hand and takes a step forward toward the veterinarian. "I know it sounds crazy, but it could possibly change all of this."

The man's eyes fall to the floor. He releases a grunt.

"Doesn't really look like I have much of a choice, I guess." The tall man exhales loudly. "Let me draw you up a quick map or you'll never find your way out of this place."

Theresa quickly tears a page from an old book sitting on the table and pulls a short pencil from her pocket that's no bigger than her thumb. Her father leans over and begins to sketch us a quick, mazelike outline of the tunnels.

The door above us smashes open with a loud crash. The monitor shows the men rushing in with their guns already drawn.

"We gotta go!" Rollins announces. He snatches the piece of paper out of the man's hand before he can complete it. "Thank you for everything that you've done, but we've gotta move."

Theresa awkwardly grabs Riley's hand and pulls us down a short tunnel.

"There's a door at the end of the hall just after it curves to the right. Make sure you seal the hatch off from the other side once everyone gets through."

"You're not coming with us?" Ria asks, surprised.

189

"Daddy won't leave. He'll defend us and this place as long as it stands."

Theresa awkwardly drops Riley's hand, embarrassed she was still grasping it. She turns to leave just as we hear a loud crash erupt behind us.

"Where are they?" I hear a deep voice echo down the hall. "We tracked them to this location!"

I hold my breath waiting for Theresa's father to give us up.

"I don't know what you're talking about?" the veterinarian shouts back, clearly wanting us to hear him. "What people? My daughter and I just came down here to escape the heat."

I watch everyone else exit through the door in front of me as the arguing down the opposite end of the tunnel continues. I place one leg through the opening, just as a gunshot sounds in the other room.

"Daddy!"

I halfway turn around, when I remember what's at stake. I shake my head knowing I have to choose between saving the future or the two individuals who went out of their way to save us.

I bite down hard on my bottom lip.

"Come on, Nic!" Ria says in a low voice. She turns back around to face me.

One look into her eyes and I'm propelled through the doorway. I turn to seal off the exit when a second gunshot echoes down the tunnel.

I release two deep breaths as I turn the wheel and seal off the hatch, knowing that T and her father are now both dead.

And it's all because of us.

CHAPTER 42

INCOMPLETE

"What are these Xs here?" Riley stabs the map with his index finger. His eyes are fixed on the paper, attempting to decipher it.

Rollins holds the map out in front of him and studies it. He shakes his head. "No clue, but we need to keep moving. They'll figure out how to get through that door before we make it outta here, you can bet on that."

"Whatever they are, the map shows one in this tunnel," Ria says. Her words bring us to a stop.

"Everyone just be careful," Riley says. He slips the pack off his shoulder and places it on the ground. "Those Xs could be anything—maybe even booby traps?"

As soon as the backpack makes contact with the tunnel floor, a click rings out underneath it. Riley bends down and begins digging through the bag.

"Did you hear that?" I shout as I grab Riley's arm. "Did you hear that click?"

"No one move!"Rollins yells out.

At the same time, Riley picks up the bag off the ground, releasing another click.

Boom!

A bright white light explodes from the floor and a strong, bone-crushing blast sends me flying backward into the tunnel wall. A loud ringing instantly fills my ears and blurs my vision, like someone just set off a Tocsin.

"What was that?" I hear a muffled, shaky voice call out next to me. I lift my head and concentrate on the dark shadowy figure in front of me—Ria.

I rub at the back of my head where I struck the wall.

"Are you okay?" I call out to her, once I comprehend what just happened. I sit up with a grunt and feel every aching bone in my body scream back at me in pain.

Ria nods. "Where's everyone else?" She glances around the tunnel. The light from the fire reflects off Ria's face, casting her skin in a copper glow.

"Rollins!" I scream as I push myself to my feet and rush toward a dark motionless shadow on the opposite end of the tunnel. I collapse to the floor next to where my brother lays. The side of his face is covered in dirt and scratches. I check the pulse on the side of his neck—he's still alive. I nod my head a couple of times and breathe a sigh of relief. "He's okay."

"Riley's not," Ria answers. She squats down next to the lab tech and holds up his amputated arm. A bundle of multicolored wires stick out of the end that was attached to his body.

"Riley was a robot?" I scrunch up my face in disbelief.

"That would explain why he always had an answer for everything," Ria says. She bends back down and places the arm by the remains of Riley's body. "Dreadnaught must have programmed him for all the possibilities."

Rollins slowly moves his head and opens his eyes. A large gash runs down the side of his head and cuts through his hair, with a thin trail of blood running down his neck.

"What happened?" he asks with a grunt. His eyes seem lost, as if he's unsure of where he's at.

"I think it was a booby trap." I bend over to help my brother up. "I guess T's father set it up for intruders sneaking in the back way."

"Now we know what the Xs stand for," Kingston says. He makes his way over to the rest of the group and dusts himself off, showing no signs of being hurt.

"Your brother doesn't look good," Ria says, walking toward us. "We need to find him a Healer." The light from the fire continues to flicker off the walls and her sullen face.

"Healer's haven't been invented yet," Rollins says. His dull voice shows no emotion. "Besides, I'm fine. We just need to keep moving. If we don't succeed, all of this would be for nothing."

As I look between Rollins and Ria, I shake my head in frustration.

"All of these deaths *are* for nothing!" I step forward into the glowing light. "Everyone that we've come across has either ended up dead or seriously injured. Thank goodness Riley wasn't human or his blood would be on our hands too. This has to end—all of this has to end!"

"And the only way for that to happen is for us to reach the lecture hall and somehow convince Dad to bury his research. Destroy it." Rollins grabs my shoulder with his good hand. "The Government cannot find out about the Tele program. It's up to us to prevent that from happening."

My brother stands inches away from me. I can feel his heavy breath across my surly face, waiting for a response.

"So, we push on," Rollins continues, leaving no room for objections. He bends over to pick up Riley's lighter off the ground and hands it to me. "We push on and find the lecture hall."

* * *

"Looks like the map just ends here," Rollins says. My brother grips the sketched piece of paper in one hand, while holding his healing arm across his chest.

I stand over his shoulder inspecting it. "Looks incomplete. And we don't know if there are any other traps along the way."

Kingston and Ria join me and my brother.

"We have to be close, right?" Ria says with her voice clearly full of doubt. "We've been walking for hours. This place is like a maze."

"Just seems like it since it's so dark," Kingston says. His voice shows no signs of excitement. The flame from the lighter in my hand lights up his facial tattoo. "Everything just looks the same, like we're walking around in circles."

"Shh…," Rollins hushes us. "You hear that?"

"Sounds like running water," I quickly answer. I hold the lighter out further, like it will help me hear better.

"There's no way these pipes still run," Ria says, again with uncertainty in her small voice. She turns and stares into the black darkness behind us.

The shallow stream of water at our feet slowly begins to move. A swift current ripples down the tunnel like a natural spring river. I bend over and wave the lighter across my boots. The once low water level has risen halfway up my shoes, almost reaching the tips of my dangling shoestrings.

"We have a problem here," I say. The tone of my voice surprisingly stays level.

Everyone's eyes shift from the light to Rollins, again looking for an answer.

He shakes his head.

I squat back down and wave the lighter over my feet. I watch the water level continue to climb; our boots are now almost completely submerged.

"Someone must have turned the main water lines on," Rollins announces. He spins around to face the group. "They know we made it out and that we're still down here. I don't..."

The loud hum of rushing water drowns out whatever my brother says next. Everyone turns to face the unsettling sound.

I step forward and hold the lighter out in front of the group.

"I don't see anything," I say nervously.

"Wave!" Kingston shouts. His voice erupts over the hum. He holds both hands out in front of him in an attempt to brace himself.

A giant wave filling the entire tunnel comes speeding toward us. Everyone shoots their arms out in front of them. I drop the lighter to my feet, and as result, blanket the tunnel in darkness once again.

The powerful wave crashes into us like a MagneTrain moving at top speed. I feebly fight the tide as it violently sweeps me down the dark, winding tunnel with the others.

CHAPTER 43

DEPOSITED

I'm shot like a canon headfirst out of a drainage pipe, sending me airborne for at least five seconds. My body glides through the sunlit air with my arms and legs spread apart, before freefalling into a large body of dark, frothy water below.

I break through the shiny surface with the pain of crashing into a cement wall. The momentum pushes me deep down through the saltwater. As my feet search for the bottomless floor, I'm able to make out the sound of three splashing explosions above me, one after the other. Dark shadows break the surface, like someone firing a gun repeatedly over me into the water.

One of the three shadows—the largest—drops like an anchor, sinking quickly and out of control.

Rollins.

I put my long arms to work and force myself to swim. The saltwater stings my open eyes, as I paddle upward and grab onto my struggling brother with one arm and pull the two of us up the final ten feet.

We break through the rough surface and Rollins chokes out a loud cough, spitting out a mouthful of water.

"Didn't think you two made it!" Ria calls out. She swims over to the two of us, along with Kingston. Between the two of them, they keep Rollins afloat. His face has grown grey and his eyes are half closed.

"What did that veterinarian give you?" I say, attempting to stay afloat myself. "What are you on?"

"He just needs rest, mate," Kingston answers for him. "We need to get him ashore and into a bed somewhere."

"I'm gonna complete this mission," Rollins murmurs. He forces himself to come back to life. My brother widens his eyes and pushes Kingston off of him to prove that he's okay. He releases a series of coughs before swimming toward the shore. "Doesn't look too far. I can make it."

I stay on one side of him, and Kingston on the other, until we get close enough to land to stand up. By the time we reach the beach, all four of us collapse in a loud grunt. The waves crash over us as we lay exhausted on the wet sand.

"I could go to sleep out here," Ria says next to me in the sand. She grabs my hand and pulls me closer to her.

Hsssss

My head jerks up to discover a large sea gator stretched out only a few feet away. Its mouth is partially open with rows of tiny, sharp, yellowish teeth glistening in the sunlight. The large black reptile hisses again as it inches forward on its four stubby, clawed legs.

"No one move," Rollins says through his teeth. "If we don't move, it can't find us. They are only able to sense movement."

"What, you think it'll get bored and give up? I'll tell you right now, I'm not gonna be bait for a sea gator." Kingston slowly pushes himself up off the sand. His eyes stay fixed on the large reptile.

"Kingston, don't move!" Rollins screams back at him.

The six foot gator mimics Kingston's moves and takes a few more short steps toward us. Its two dark, beaming eyes shift back and forth from Kingston to me, as if it's trying to decide who to devour first. The hair on the back of my neck stands up.

"Sorry, mate! Can't do it!" Kingston jumps up and dashes farther inland. The gator pounces at him and just barely misses his boot. It releases a deep barking sound, similar to a dog's growl, as it turns back around toward me.

I awkwardly roll out of the way and land on the end of the gator's tail. The reptile recoils and flicks me off, like I'm weightless. It hisses again and inches toward me, ready to attack.

I get on my hands and knees, and slowly begin to back away from the gator.

"Be careful, Nic!" Ria warns. Rollins and Ria have joined Kingston about ten yards away. "Don't make any sudden movements!"

"Easy for you to say," I utter to myself, drowned out by the waves that continue to crash onto the beach. "What are you waiting for?" I yell back, this time louder. I refuse to look away from the gator. "Someone do something!"

I feel a strong force, like a gust of wind rush over my head. The invisible power lifts the sea gator up in the air and sends it flying at least fifty yards the opposite way down the beach. It lands with a thud on its back near the water and flips itself back over on its feet. The gator releases another loud bark in our direction, before it scurries into the dark water. An incoming wave washes over the reptile's footprints, erasing any evidence of the animal on the beach.

"Welcome to the Atlantic, mate," Kingston says with a smirk. He reaches a hand out and helps me to my feet. "Where the sea will swallow the human world whole if it gets the chance."

"Literally," Ria adds. She stands behind me in a lax martial arts stance.

She wipes a thin layer of sand off the side of my face.

"That was way too close," I say, still trying to catch my breath. My body trembles.

An aerial drone soars through the sky and puts a halt to our conversation.

My eyes follow the drone as it heads toward Sol. "Think they're here for us?" The aircraft disappears into the sector.

My brother stands tall behind me. "There's no telling. You'd think if they were they would have fired at us." He gazes toward the sky. "Either way, we need to complete our mission and then get back home."

"What do you think we should do?" Kingston asks.

"Well, it doesn't seem like we were flushed too far down the pipe," Rollins begins. "T's father didn't have time to mark where the lecture hall was on the map, so I'm assuming it has to be somewhere near here or he would have sent us in a different direction."

"Yeah, that makes sense," Ria agrees. "It has to be close."

I point toward the area of the sector where large buildings stretch upward into the clouds. "It has to be in downtown Sol. They would need it to be in a central location for the rich who will attend the event."

Everyone in the group agrees, knowing it's as good of a place as any to start our search.

We trudge off down the beach and head toward downtown Sol—a place we know all too well, even if we are stuck in the past.

CHAPTER 44

INSIDE JOB

"I can't believe it," Rollins mumbles to himself as he peers at the heavily guarded entrance of the lecture hall in downtown Sol. He hugs the edge of the tall building across the street. "Look who it is."

I follow my brother's gaze to the front entrance and spot a young man dressed in a khaki-colored military uniform laughing with a large group of uniformed men. Red ropes block off the main walkway leading up to the front doors, redirecting patrons through a security checkpoint before entering the hall. Two soldiers stand on either side of the glass doors checking IDs.

"Commander Lee?" Ria slides closer to me as she finds the commander in the center of the crowd. Her lip quivers. "What's he doing here?"

"We all know why he's here," my brother answers. He exhales roughly. "We can't let him get anywhere near Dad." His eyes shift to meet mine. "We all know the outcome."

Kingston runs up to us from behind a parked car, noticeably out of breath.

"There's less than a handful of guards in the back—may be a better bet than the front." Kingston steals a quick look back at the entrance. "Is that who I think it is?" He shakes his head in disbelief. "Just give me three minutes alone with Lee. He won't be a problem after that."

"If we take out Lee, there will just be another young officer who'll step into his place," Rollins says. "We have to cut the program off at the source."

"You sure you're up for this?" I say to Ria. I think of the plan my brother came up with earlier.

"She's ready," Rollins answers for her.

Ria glances over at my brother and acknowledges him. She pulls down the bill of her blue military hat and nods her head. "Ready as I'll ever be." She turns halfway toward me for a brief second and bites down on her bottom lip. Her unsure expression betrays the confidence in her voice. I reach for her, but at that very second, she turns away and dashes into the street.

As soon as she turns the corner, we follow, stealthy leaping from behind one parked car to the next. We follow Kingston's exact route until we're across the street from the back door.

I watch Ria run up to the first soldier she reaches. He stands about twenty feet away from the rear entrance, dressed in the same military blue uniform we all wear. As she approaches, the man grips the gun that's strapped across his chest. He keeps one finger on the trigger and holds out his free hand.

"Whoa!" he yells. His voice causes Ria to freeze.

"I'm so late! I'm gonna be in such big trouble! You've gotta let me through!" Ria hysterically screams at the man between breaths.

"Is that how you address your commanding officer, soldier?" The man grabs both of her arms, his face noticeably flustered. "What are you doing back here?"

"I was supposed to be inside ten minutes ago. I'm on Dr. McCready's security team!"

The commander fixes his stare on Ria for a few seconds before turning to his colleagues.

"Isn't security already set up inside?" the commanding officer calls to the three officers behind him.

"Yes, Lieutenant."

As the officer turns back to Ria, he meets her powerful fist square in the jaw. His body flies backward and smacks the side of the building with a loud thud.

"That's our signal, go, go, go!" Rollins shouts. He pushes himself up from behind the parked car and takes off in a sprint.

Kingston and I jump up too, chasing my brother across the street. Each of us seizes a single soldier, lifting them up into the air and rocketing them defenselessly back against the wall to join their lieutenant.

"Release us this minute!" the lieutenant orders Ria. He struggles to free himself from her invisible hold, his hands held above his head. "Who are you?"

"We're a little ahead of your time," I say, as I rush up to meet Ria. I tighten my grip on the soldier that I keep pinned against the wall. An outline of a dark puddle begins to form in the front of his pants, trailing down his left leg.

"We're not gonna hurt you," Ria says. She keeps her arm extended out in front of her and her eyes focus on the soldier who wet his pants. "It's just very important for us to get inside. You have no idea."

The lieutenant rolls his eyes, but doesn't fight it anymore. Resistance is pointless.

One at a time, we begin to disarm them and then handcuff them together using their own cuffs. Kingston snags the ID badges off their shirts and hands them out to everyone, attempting to match the person up with the man in the photo the best that he can. He gives Ria the only one with blonde hair, the youngest looking one in the group.

"Everyone ready?" Rollins asks. He pulls the slide back on his newly acquired gun.

We nod.

"Let's do this!"

Rollins reaches the back door and yanks it open. Kingston moves out in front of him with his gun, sweeping it across the narrow entrance as he steps inside. He leads the three of us down the back, narrow hallway with Rollins bringing up the rear.

We pass locked doors on both sides of the hallway, along with glowing digital photographs of various men and women giving speeches in frames on the wall. Every few seconds the pictures change to an image of a new speaker.

I am distracted by the glowing photographs on the wall when I spot a young version of my father talking—the same image that was playing on the electronic billboard. One of my hands drops to my side to feel the bulge of the NoMad's flash drive in my pocket. What can be on the drive that's so important to send some kids back with it? Is it still even in working condition after taking a ride down the giant sewer water slide earlier? What if the drive doesn't work and we get stuck in this time period forever? I take a big gulp and try to choke down some of the fear forming a knot in my throat.

The hallway ends at a single door with a hint of light sneaking out underneath. Kingston stops a couple of feet behind the door and reaches out for the handle. "Be ready for anything, mates. We don't know what kind of security—"

The door swings opens and slams into Kingston. The force knocks him off balance and up against a wall, dislodging the weapon from his hands. He fumbles the gun in an attempt to catch it, but it falls to his feet.

The dumbfounded soldier in the doorway freezes, startled at finding us in the hallway unexpectedly. The man's eyes shift from one person to the next.

"Hey buddy," my brother says with a friendly smile on his face.

The man reaches for his gun, but Ria is faster. She shoves the barrel of her weapon into the soldier's face.

"Don't even think about it!"

"What's the meaning of this?" the man raises his voice. "Identify yourself, soldier!" He reaches for Ria's ID card as I push myself into the room. I shove the end of my handgun under the soldier's chin.

"Don't touch her," I growl slowly as I dig the muzzle further into his skin.

The man's attention shifts from Ria to me. He slowly raises his hands over his head. He has a thick dark mustache, a buzz cut, and his nose is slightly off center. He's dressed in a khaki military uniform, like the men out front, but he looks older and more distinguished for some reason.

"Now, there's no need for that," he says calmly. The man gestures toward the door to invite us inside. "There's plenty of room for everybody."

I shove the soldier into a nearby chair. Behind him, I spot a younger man, probably in his early twenties with a full head of brown hair and a beard to match. The man stands awkwardly alone in the far corner of the room and is dressed in an uncomfortable-looking dark suit with an aqua blue tie. He looks incredibly nervous compared to our captive soldier. He holds a tablet in his hands with a white lit up screen.

"I don't know what in the world you think you're doing," the soldier says with a strangely accented drawl that I can't place. "If you think you're gonna escape, I've got men all over this place. It's over."

"We just came here to talk, mate," Kingston says. He grabs a chair in the opposite corner of the room and drags it loudly across the floor, placing it inches away from the soldier. He turns the chair around and casually sits down backward in it, propping his long dangly arms across the backrest.

"Well, talk," the older soldier demands. "What're you waiting for?"

"We didn't come here to talk to you," Rollins says. My brother enters the room and closes the door behind him. He swings his strapped gun around to his back. "We came here to talk to him."

CHAPTER 45

MY FATHER'S SONS

"Remove this piece of trash," Rollins calmly utters. His eyes bore into the older uniformed soldier before him. He grabs the man by the front of his shirt and yanks him closer. "I'm assuming you're here to purchase something?"

"That's none of your business, son," the man spits back. He knocks my brother's hand away and smoothes back down the front of his uniform. "Why don't you cut your losses before you do something you're really going to regret?"

"You don't even know the half of it." Rollins leans forward and reads the officer's ID card on the front of his shirt, "Commander Cullen." He rips off the little plastic card hanging from the man's shirt pocket and slides it into his own. "You won't need this now, since we all know your name."

Rollins turns toward Ria and Kingston. "Take the commander out into the hall. If he moves, shoot him." He gives the orders flippantly, like he really doesn't care what happens to the man.

Ria and Kingston escort the man into the hallway and shut the door behind them.

The room grows quiet and thick with awkwardness. The man is looking down at the floor, refusing to leave the corner, let alone acknowledge us.

"Dr. McCready?" I ask across the small room at the man who is supposed to be our father one day.

His head snaps up with a surprised expression, shocked that I know his name. He's the spitting image of my older brother. He always has been—or that Rollins is the spitting image of him. They both have the same eyes, the same chin. They could be brothers.

Our father raises a single eyebrow, still clutching the tablet in his arms. "What do you want with me? I'm just a scientist. There's nothing I can do for you if you're in trouble."

"We know exactly who you are," Rollins mutters. He stands completely still next to me. "We're here to stop you from selling your new vaccine to the Government."

"TeleVox?" he exclaims. "But the vaccine will help eliminate neurodegenerative diseases before they can destroy someone's body." He steps forward and leaves his corner for the first time since we entered the room. "Imagine a world where no one has to suffer from any terrible diseases that affect the spinal cord. And the ones who are affected will be able to solely use their minds to live independently. TeleVox will open so many doors in the medical world."

"And selling it to the highest bidder, the Government, was part of your original plan?" My brother's voice gets louder as he completes the question.

The younger version of our father glances toward the closed door. His eyes tell us what he's thinking before he opens his mouth. "But Commander Cullen promises that they'll be able to mass produce the vaccine so those in need can receive it. Can you imagine ridding this world of these ugly diseases and many more like it?"

Rollins opens his mouth to answer, but I cut him off.

"Can you imagine a world where teenagers are kidnapped and removed from their homes? From their families?" I step forward and glare at our father. "Can you imagine a world full of peril and destruction where these same kidnapped teens are forced to fight in an army against their will?"

The room grows silent again. I catch Rollins staring at me out of the corner of my eye. He's nodding his head in agreement.

"What are you talking about? Have you not been outside lately? Take a look around. It can't get any worse than it already is."

"You have no idea what you're talking about," Rollins says with a much calmer voice than before. "The Government doesn't care about curing any disease that affects the spinal cord. All they care about is starting up the Tele program."

"The Tele program?" Our father scrunches up his face as he digests the words. He then shakes his head, ready to dismiss our plea. "I don't have time for this, neither does Commander Cullen. Tell them to bring him back in here immediately."

Neither Rollins nor I move a muscle. The door doesn't open, and Ria and Kingston do not bring the uniformed commander back into the room. I steal another glance over at my brother. His face doesn't tell me what to do, so I improvise.

I extend my arm and line my palm up with our father. I focus on the tablet that his hands are wrapped around. The lit screen rips itself free from his grasp and floats swiftly across the room into my waiting hand.

Our father's eyes grow large, unable to accept what just happened. He opens his mouth to form a sentence, but nothing comes out.

"It can't be," he finally manages to squeeze out. "Impossible."

"And we've never had any of the diseases you were talking about, nor were we ever asked to be injected with your TeleVox vaccine," Rollins says. He glares across the room. "We're what people will call Teles."

"Impossible," our father declares again from across the room. "How can any of this be possible? The only test subjects that have had the vaccine are lab animals. TeleVox has yet to be injected into a human subject."

"Where we're from," I jump in, "everyone's injected with the vaccine. Please, you can't sell your findings."

Our father takes a few more steps out of his corner. "And you can do that too?" he questions my brother. "Or is it just him?" His eyes find me, before darting back to Rollins.

Rollins holds his hand up and brings a rolling chair across the length of the room.

"Both of us have been infected." I step forward to hand him back his tablet. "Please, you can't do this. You have to destroy the vaccine."

My dad tilts his head to the side. "Destroy the vaccine? TeleVox? It's my life's work."

"There's no other way," Rollins adds. "You can save mankind."

A gunshot goes off on the other side of the door.

"Ria!"

CHAPTER 46

TRUST

The door flies open and Commander Cullen and Ria fall into the room. The commander holds Ria by the back of her head with a single hand and presses the end of a handgun to her temple.

"I need all available security to the back room," he shouts into a handheld radio that he snatches off his belt. He throws Ria down on the floor. "We have a breach." He makes eye contact with Rollins. "You know you screwed up, right?"

I lift my palm and cleanly yank the gun out of Cullen's grasp. His head jerks as he watches the weapon float across the room and into my hand.

"What?" Commander Cullen says with a gasp. "Who…what are you?"

Kingston runs into the room. He has a deep laceration across his forehead with a trickle of blood running down between his eyes. He grabs Cullen by the shoulders and wrestles him back out into the hallway, shoving him down onto the ground. The door on the opposite end of the hallway opens as a group of soldiers tries to rush inside to aide their commander.

Rollins lifts his hand and slams the door of the room shut. The room is now sealed off from the hallway. Within seconds, pounding begins on the back side of the door.

"Open up this instant!" the commander orders. His loud, booming voices cuts through the solid barrier. "Dr. McCready, open this door!"

Our father's stare flickers from Rollins to me, his mouth slightly agape.

"I don't understand any of this." He scratches at the side of his head and looks me up and down. "When you said, '*where you're from*', what did you mean?"

"Even if we could explain it, you would never believe us," Rollins says. "You just have to trust us on this."

"Trust some strangers who broke-in and are telling me to destroy my life's research? I think you owe me something more than just, *trust us*."

Cullen slams himself up against the backside of the door. The door vibrates with each strike, but holds strong. Multiple voices shout out, demanding the door to be opened.

"We have to get outta here," Rollins says in a panic. His eyes find mine. "That door isn't gonna hold much longer." He motions for the gun, so I hand it to him. He grabs our father around his upper arm and drags him toward the door that leads to the lecture hall stage.

"I'm not going anywhere with you," he yells, feebly attempting to hold his ground.

A gunshot rings out behind us in the hall. Our father jumps and closes his mouth.

"We don't have time for this!" I swing open the door with my hand. "We'll explain later."

The back door opens as we exit the small room. Ria turns, and in one motion, kicks toward the group of incoming soldiers. Her telekinetic wave catches the lead soldier under the chin, knocking him back into the group like dominoes. She slams the door in their faces, creating a temporary hold, at best.

We rush onto the main stage that overlooks the lecture hall. A single podium with a microphone sits in the center of the floor. The lecture hall is well lit with rows of seats that stretch all the way to the back of the room. Most of the seats are filled, each containing a confused set of eyes staring back at us. My brother and father jump down from the edge of the stage. Before anyone can stop them, Rollins yanks our father down one of the aisles that leads toward the back of the spacious room.

An armed soldier steps in front of Rollins and our father. His gun is strapped across his back. When he spots my father, he reaches over his shoulder for his weapon.

I raise my hand and shove the soldier out of the way. He stumbles backward and trips over a spectator's leg, sending him sprawling to the floor.

I grab Ria's hand and pull her up the aisle with Kingston not far behind. We push and shove our way through the crowd in the lobby and head toward the front doors.

Outside, soldiers still stand around casually talking to one another, mixed in with presumably wealthy non-Government citizens. An SUV pulls up to the front of the building and the driver steps out dressed in a dark gray suit. A woman with long blonde hair opens the passenger-side door and joins the man, grabbing his outstretched arm. He reaches out to hand the valet boy his keys, leaving the driver-side door open for the next driver.

Rollins knocks the valet boy out of the way and grabs the keys. He shoves our father in through the open door and pushes him over to the passenger seat. My brother climbs in after him and closes the door. Ria, Kingston, and I all jump into the back seat.

Rollins cranks up the SUV. Loud music blasts from the speakers as we pull onto the road. I watch as a group of soldiers rush out through the front doors of the lecture hall and begin to fire at our vehicle.

"Why are they shooting at us?" our father shouts. He ducks his head down toward the dash.

The rear window, along with the back of the SUV, absorbs the bullets.

"Do you really think they care about you?" Kingston says from the back seat. "All they care about is your research."

Our father lifts his head as he digests the information.

"Who are you?" He looks at each of us individually, before landing back on Rollins sitting behind the wheel.

I stare at the reflection of my brother's expressionless face in the rearview mirror.

"We were sent back from the future to stop TeleVox—to stop you from handing over your research to the Government."

CHAPTER 47

FLASH

Rollins races through downtown Sol, sliding around corners and blowing through lights. The interior of the vehicle grows ominously silent. A pair of Hawks appear out of nowhere in the air above us, slicing through a large puffy cloud to our rear.

The lead drone fires a missile at our SUV and strikes a building on the passenger side of the street. Rollins takes the next left, but the unmanned aircrafts follow. The second Hawk fires, but also misses. It hits an abandoned car that we pass leaving a fiery crater in its place.

"Look out!" our father screams. He points ahead as if Rollins can't see the giant hole in the road.

My brother rips the wheel, swerving into the other lane, and maneuvers us around other abandoned cars littered across the road. He takes a few more turns putting us back on the main strip.

"Take the tunnel," Kingston calls from the back seat. A barrage of bullets fires at us from behind, drowning out the rest of Kingston's instructions. The rear window shatters and spews glass all over us in the back seat.

"Not sure we can make it," Rollins says. He looks at us in the rearview mirror before flashing back to the road. He dodges another group of abandoned cars.

"I don't understand any of this," our father mutters to himself. His fingers dig into the sides of his seat. "Why would Commander Cullen order this strike?"

"That's what we've been trying to tell you," Ria exclaims. She pulls a small piece of glass out of her hair and leans forward. She grabs our father's shoulder. "Dr. McCready, you have to listen to us. Cullen is dangerous. We had a commander just as ruthless as him in our own time period."

I watch my brother's face tenses up as we approach the mouth of the tunnel at the end of the road. The tunnel runs under the Austral River, which cuts through downtown Sol and leads out to the Atlantic Ocean. Rollins jerks the wheel sharply around a parked car in the middle of the road and clips the open driver side door ripping it off.

"We just have to reach the tunnel!" Rollins shouts. Another rocket fires at our rear and flies right over us, striking the top of the tunnel entrance. A large chunk of cement from the tunnel roof breaks off and falls down onto the center of the road.

We swerve into the other lane and enter the dark underpass. More chunks of the ceiling fall, making sizable obstacles in the shaking road. Dim lamps on either side of the passage illuminate the tunnel as we continue to race down the covered road. I turn around and watch the entrance become sealed by fallen debris.

Rollins slams on the brakes. He stares forward at the scene developing in front of us. At the opposite end of the long, narrow tunnel, members of the Government's Army have set up a barricade consisting of several military vehicles and armed drones.

"We're trapped!"

We watch my father, expecting him to simply open the door and exit the cab of the vehicle. This is his chance to walk free.

But he doesn't move.

My father shakes his head.

"I've already turned all my work over to Cullen and his men," he admits. "Even if what you say is true—about the future—there's not much I can do."

Rollins turns off the engine. The cab is dead silent.

"You have a computer," I say, as my voice cracks. "You have to be able to do something."

Our father looks down at the tablet in his hands. He touches the center of the screen and brings it to life.

I lean forward and the flash drive in my pocket pokes me in the leg. "If you don't believe us, look at this." I grab the small storage device. I have no clue what's on it, but as important as it is to the NoMads, it must be serious. The future depends on it. "Plug this in."

Rollins grabs the flash drive out of my hand. "We don't know what's on it. We don't know what it could do."

"At this point," Ria says, leaning forward in her seat, "what do we have to lose? Just let him plug it in."

My brother stares out the windshield at the military barricade about a hundred yards away. He shakes his head and lowers it in defeat.

"Here." Rollins hands our father the flash drive.

He plugs it into the side of his tablet and clicks on the image of a blackbird that pops up in the middle of the screen. Random numbers and letters fill the computer screen.

"Where did you say you got this from?"

"We didn't," Rollins says and looks over toward the screen.

"The people who sent us here, they gave it to us," I say, jumping into the conversation. My brother glares at me. I shrug my shoulders.

Our father nods his head. "Well, whoever gave this to you means harm." He lifts his empty gaze from the tablet in his hands to the drones stationed up ahead. "This code would floor all flying drones, freeze all land drones—not to mention crash the GovNet stock exchange. This little file could end all of civilization as we know it."

No one says a word.

"What were your instructions? What were you supposed to do with the file?"

"We were told to install it onto a Government computer," I answer after a short pause. "It's our signal to be sent back home."

CHAPTER 48

FAIL

"You have to the count of ten to exit the vehicle," a loud, booming voice informs us at the mouth of the tunnel.

The silhouette of a uniformed man stands off to the side of a cluster of FootSoldiers. He holds a megaphone to his lips and pauses to see if he needs to continue.

"Ten...nine...eight..."

The first line of FootSoldiers begins to march. These drones are from the first generation of FootSoldiers, moving more stiff and mechanical than the current ones back home. Pairs of red glowing eyes sadistically flashes at us through the windshield of the vehicle.

My father begins to open the door, which almost stops the march of drones. Kingston lifts his weapon, making my dad raise his free hand. He keeps his other hand on the door handle and turns to Kingston.

"We both know you're not going to use that. Put the gun down." His voice sounds calm, confident. This is the dad that both Rollins and I know. He continues to open the door the rest of the way and exits the SUV. Our father makes eye contact with my brother for a split second, before moving toward the line of FootSoldiers.

"What now, mate?" Kingston leans forward, addressing my brother.

Rollins wipes his forehead with the back of his hand. His gun rests on his lap. "Is there really a choice?" My brother's voice rises out of frustration. "We're trapped. We have no one else coming to save us. No food or water. No supplies. We've failed. There's literally no other place to run. And now the future's doomed." He lets his head fall back on the headrest and closes his eyes.

We stay silent. The sound of my brother's heavy breathing is the only sound that that fills the vehicle's cab.

Discouraged, I look at the empty front passenger seat. The tablet remains, but the flash drive is missing. Why would he take the drive?

My head snaps up and I watch my father pass through the line of frozen drones with ease. As soon as he's clear, the FootSoldiers return to life and continue their march forward. Their heavy feet rise and fall in unison, banging into the asphalt road underneath. The drones were built to battle, but even more—to intimidate the common citizen.

My leg begins to shake on its own, matching the rhythm of their footsteps.

Quietly, Rollins opens the door. The sudden movement forces the commanded FootSoldiers to freeze again. Their line stretches horizontally across the width of the tunnel. They raise their guns, each one lining their weapon up with our vehicle.

"I give up." Rollins raises his arms. He leaves the driver's side door open. "Don't shoot."

Defeated, I watch my brother give himself up, before opening my own door. Ria, Kingston, and I all follow my brother's lead and exit the vehicle one at a time.

"Freeze," the man with the bullhorn orders.

A handful of FootSoldiers break the line and begin to march toward us. We are pushed up against the tunnel wall and are handcuffed. The drones lead us the rest of the way down the empty tunnel toward the mixed cavalry of both drones and human soldiers who wait for us at the entrance.

"Almost made it." Commander Cullen greets us as he stands carefully protected behind a wall of his heavily armed men. He glares at us. "You four are under arrest for murder and kidnapping…amongst other charges." His eyes narrow as the left corner of his mouth curls up in a menacing smirk. "Bag 'em up, boys. We're taking them in."

A thick cloth bag is yanked over my head from behind and I'm shoved into a waiting vehicle that speeds off the second my door is slammed shut.

CHAPTER 49

INTERROGATION

Without warning, the chair that I sit in is loudly dragged across the floor. The bag on my face is pulled off, and I am blinded by an intense white light shining down from above.

"Where am I?" I scream. I'm forced to squint to shield my eyes from the bright light. My hands are tied together behind my back. I flex my arms to test the durability of the tie around my wrists, but the plastic cuffs refuse to budge. If anything, they tighten.

I hear the person behind me breathing before I see them.

A uniformed man dressed in blue walks in my direction from a corner I cannot see. The young man, possibly in his early twenties, walks across the small room and pulls a second chair out of the dark. He slowly scrapes it across the cement floor and places it a few feet in front of where I sit. The man glares at me the entire time. He has short brown hair, almost shaved, and stubble for a beard dotted across his lower face and neck. His nose has a large hump sprouting out at the bridge, as if it's been broken countless times.

"Where's my brother—my friends?"

The man ignores my question as his eyes fall to a tablet in his lap. With a flick of his finger, he scrolls through the pages on the screen at a rapid pace.

"Let's start with your name." The man clears his throat and glances up for a response. His eyes find mine, holding them there.

I straighten my posture and stare back at the man with my mouth clamped shut. I refuse to answer him, nor look away.

The man nods his head and forms a crooked smile, acknowledging my defiance.

"We already know who you are and all about your mission." The uniformed man continues smiling, as if he thinks it's helping the situation. "Your friends...and your brother have all talked." He turns to the side and motions toward the only door in the room. "You're the last one."

I glance over at the closed door.

"If you've already talked to them," I begin, before taking a pause, "then why are you in here questioning me?" I tilt my head to the side and raise my eyebrows with a sarcastically inquisitive face.

The man sits back in his seat and straightens out his back. He releases a deep exhale. "Well, we have to check everything out. You can understand that." The man's voice seems calmer, less intense, but his eyes say different. His stare doesn't break mine. "All I'm asking is for you to tell me your name."

I look at the floor.

"So, that's how it's going to be?" He puts his free hand on his knee and holds the tablet with his other. "Your friends all resisted too, at first. That didn't last long though...but I understand where you're coming from. You wanna play the role of a hero. That's fine." He nods his head and forms a smile. "I was hoping to have some more fun today."

With that, the man gets up from his seat and exits the room. The door shuts with a loud click. I flex my muscles and try to break through the thin plastic cuffs around my wrists, but again, they only get tighter. I grimace as the taut plastic rips into my skin. I can feel a trail of liquid, either blood or sweat, running down my hands.

The door clicks open and the same uniformed man walks in wheeling in a small table with a thin surgical paper cloth draped over it. He pushes the cart to the center of the room and places it between the two chairs. When his face passes the light, a faded scar is highlighted across his forehead, hooking down over the corner of his right eye.

I swallow.

The man glances up, as if he's able to smell fear in the air. "Any guesses what's underneath here?" He shakes his head in a mocking way. "No?"

The man dramatically rips the surgical cloth off the table and reveals a tray full of knives—at least a dozen of them—all ranging in sizes and placed in order of smallest to largest.

"Surprise," the man says sarcastically.

I swallow again.

The man's eyes light up as he scans the tray of glittering weapons. He makes a show of selecting one of the largest knives in the set. He holds it in front of his face, allowing the light to reflect off the surface.

"This will only hurt a bit...but if the pain is too intense," he pauses. There's a knock at the door. The man halfway turns, annoyed he is being interrupted midsentence.

Another uniformed man with a shaved head opens the door. He speaks in an unintelligible, low voice with my interrogator.

"This will only take a second," he says to me. "I wouldn't want to keep you waiting."

He puts the knife back on the table and exits the room.

My eyes shoot over to the tray and then back to the door.

I have to do something. I can't just sit here and let Captain Crazy cut me up. If I can just turn myself a little, I can levitate one of those knives into my hands.

I push down with as much strength as I can muster, using every muscle in my legs, and try to hop to the side—only to instead, tip over and crash to the ground. The chair flips out from underneath and lands on top of me. I let out a small groan. I look toward the door. I can hear two male voices conversing outside.

I roll myself around with my hands and feet still locked together, and find the bottom end of the cart holding the tray.

I've never levitated anything before without directing it first with my hand. It's my only shot.

I focus on its center.

The tray lifts off the cart and immediately tips to the side, crashing down onto the floor. I find the closest normal looking knife and I slide it over to me. I grab the handle and begin to slice through the plastic that doesn't seem so thin anymore. I rip my bindings apart, before working on the cuffs on my feet.

I push myself up and dart for the exit. As soon as I reach out for the doorknob, the door opens and Captain Crazy returns.

"Did you really think it would be that easy?"

The man smiles as he reaches for a knife on the floor a few feet in front of him. "Now, sit down before you make me really angry!"

CHAPTER 50

UNEXPECTED

The smile on his face has vanished.

I look down at the chair flipped over on its side in the center of the room. A small, circular dark spot has stained the floor just behind the toppled chair. I glance down at my wrists, now outlined in crimson blood where the cuffs once dug into my skin.

"What are you waiting for—pick it up!" the man orders, standing almost on top of me.

My shaking hand reaches out for the chair and the man kicks it a couple of feet away. The chair spins around and the leg strikes me hard in the shin.

I grunt and clutch my leg.

"Did you not hear me the first time, prisoner? I said, pick up the chair!" He spits on the floor an inch away from my shoe.

I glance back at the man before reaching out for the backside of the chair. I turn it over and set it right-side up.

Without being told again, I sit back down on the chair and keep my eyes focused on the glob of spit on the floor. The man pulls out another pair of wrist ties and motions for me to put my hands together.

"It seems you have already discovered the more you try to pull free, the tighter these will get. All I want is a little information, then I'll let you go." He slides the zipcuffs over my hands and pulls them tightly together, this time in front of me.

The soldier begins to pick up the knives scattered on the ground. He studies the reflection of each weapon in the beaming light overhead, inspecting each, before placing them back down on its tray one at time. He treats the weapons as if they are delicate pieces of glass, making sure each piece is scratch-free.

"I've got nothing to say to you."

The man freezes. He looks at me as he picks the last knife up from off the floor.

There's a sharp knock at the door, really more of a pounding.

The uniformed man places the final knife back on its tray and nods his head at me. I purse my lips and clench my teeth.

He begins to walk toward the door. As he reaches for the handle, the door flies open and knocks him backward, off balance. A dark figure rushes into the room and slams into the midsection of my interrogator. The intruder runs the uniformed man into the wall behind me with a loud thud. The struggle ceases instantly.

I turn and expect to see the uniformed man standing over the intruder who is knocked out unconscious on the floor, but all I see is my father. He's standing over the man dressed in blue, out of breath.

Dad?

What's he doing here?

CHAPTER 51

FOUND

I stare down at the unconscious soldier laying spread eagle on the floor, before looking over at my father. I open my mouth to form a sentence, but nothing comes out. Why would he sell us out but then come back to rescue me?

"Here," he says, grabbing my hands. He father holds out a knife that he picked up off the ground. The blade slices through the ziptie with a single quick cut and releases the restraints. He holds onto one of my hands as he examines the fresh lacerations encircling my wrists. "Are you okay, son?"

I freeze. I know he isn't calling me *son* in the actual sense of the word—how could he? We don't even exist in this world.

I nod my head once and force my focus back on him.

"Then come on, we gotta move." He drops my hand. "They had to have realized I've escaped by now. I snuck away from the lab a couple of floors down by sending the guard out on a food run to the cafeteria."

My father grabs me by the shirt sleeve and pulls me to my feet. He leads the way to the door before turning back.

"What's your name anyway?"

"Nic…Nicholas. My friends call me Nic though."

"Alright Nicholas, as soon as I open the door, sprint across the hallway. If you hesitate even the slightest, it could cost you your life. I will deny all of this if you're caught."

I nod my head, looking at the floor between us. I'm having a hard time making eye contact with the younger version of my dad as he barks out instructions to me. It's just too much.

"There's an exit at the end of the hallway that leads to the staircase," he continues. "Go down one floor and look for the room that's labeled SECURITY. Don't enter; I'll meet you there."

My head shoots up. "What do you mean, you'll meet me there?"

"There's something I have to take care of first—some documents I have to get rid of. Plus, it'll be better if we split up. There's less of a chance that we'll be caught. If anyone spots the two of us together, it's over. Just get down to the room. You'll see the importance once you're there, Nicholas."

Before I can argue, he opens the door. Without looking, I dash out of the room and run as fast as I can down the long hallway. I keep my eyes on the approaching wall at the end of my path and block everything else out. A door opens, and immediately I shoot my hand up in mid-stride, as if I'm a robot or a drone. Before the man dressed in a white lab coat can fully exit, he's shot backward. His head hits the wall behind him, knocking him unconscious.

I find the door labeled STAIRCASE and push it open. An alarm blares the second the door is cracked open. I propel myself down a flight of stairs, jumping three steps at a time. I grab the handle to the door on the next level down and it won't budge. It's locked.

I pound on the door with an open palm out of frustration and grit my teeth. I take a few steps back and aim my hand at the silver handle.

Just as I feel the handle begin to give, the door opens as another man dressed in a white lab coat attempts to exit. The wave of telekinetic force rushes over him and knocks the surprised man back across the narrow hallway. He hits the wall behind him, knocking him out cold too.

I lunge forward through the opening before the door closes, and take off down the hallway. The majority of the doors have been left wide-open, exposing empty rooms.

At the very end of the hallway, one door remains closed. I can spot some writing under the single window in the center.

SECURITY.

This is the place. I turn back around in hopes of seeing my dad, but no one's there. Even the man that I shot backward on the opposite end of the hallway is gone. I guess he wasn't completely knocked out.

I'm all alone.

I turn back toward the window in the door and peer inside.

A wall of monitors runs across the far side of the small room. Two chairs are pulled out from a desk under the row of televisions, as if the occupants were recently made to exit. Each black and white screen is broadcasting a different prison cell that contains one or two people.

I squint my eyes. The monitor located in the middle of the wall shows a male prisoner that resembles Rollins and another person whom I cannot make out, seated on the edge of a cot with their back to the camera.

I look over to the next monitor.

Ria!

My hand reaches for the handle in front of me. It's locked.

"Hey!" I feel a hand grab me on the shoulder.

I instinctively fire my elbow back and catch the person behind me under the chin. I turn around and look down at my dad laid out on his back. His eyes are closed and his head is lolled to the side.

Did I just knock out my own father?

CHAPTER 52

LAB WORK

I peer through the window in the middle of the door again before squatting down by my father's head and shake his sleeved forearm.

No response.

I glance back down the long, narrow hallway behind me. It's empty.

I grab him by the sides of his face and shake his head. I slap his cheek, trying to wake him up—still no response.

I glance back down the hallway again as a door opens on the opposite end, allowing multiple dark figures to enter. One points down the hall toward me and yells something causing the rest of the group to break into a sprint.

"Da—!" I start to yell without thinking. "Josiah! Wake up!" I slap the side of his face as hard as I can, propelling his entire body over at least a foot. He blinks his eyes, opening them in confusion.

"Come on!" I grunt and yank him to his feet.

He pulls a keycard out of his pocket with another man's face on it and scans the locked door. A click rings out long enough for my dad to pull the door open, and for me to shove him inside.

"Stop right there!" a booming voice calls out to us. Guns fire from about midway down the hall as I slam the door shut.

Once inside, I take a deep breath and press my back up against the wall next to the door. I turn my head and spot another hallway running parallel to the one that we just exited. A sign with an image of a stairwell is posted just before the hallway turns and is no longer visible. My father jogs across the room and sits down in one of the rolling chairs behind the desk. He types something into the keyboard and a single word pops up on the screen:

PASSWORD?

He continues typing until the word disappears from the monitor. Just like that, we're in.

His hands tap away at the keys as his eyes study the wall of screens above him. He pauses and grabs the thin black microphone in front of him that is attached to the desktop.

"Attention everyone…"

I glance up at the screen. In every monitor, faces stare back into the cameras filming them in the corners of their cells.

"At the end of this transmission, your cell will be unlocked. You'll be free. All I ask in return is to meet us in Lab 313—located one floor up from you. The stairwell will only be secure for the next three minutes. We need to put an end to this facility and what it stands for." My father pauses for a second. His eyes intensely scan the wall of screens in front of him. He rises and puts his two open palms on the edge of the desk. He shifts the top half of his body over so he can still talk into the microphone. "Who's with me?"

No one moves an inch. Their eyes continue to scrutinize the cameras, as if the last part of the transmission failed.

233

Then, one hand rockets up into the air.

Rollins. Of course my brother is ready to fight.

He slowly spins around and holds a clenched fist in the air over his head. The clear walls that make up the cells give him the ability to look around at the other prisoners.

One by one, his neighbors begin to raise their hands too.

Rollins turns back around and faces the camera. He nods his head. Everyone on screen has their arms extended out, fists raised in the air.

Behind us, out in the hallway, a soldier pounds on the glass window. A group of armed soldiers stand behind him. The lead soldier yells something, but the solid door in between us muffles his voice.

"Don't worry; the first thing I did was jam the locks." As promised, the next command my father enters releases all of the cell doors. Everyone rushes out, pushing and shoving their way down the narrow hallway until the group moves off camera.

I turn to the window and notice that the group of soldiers has moved a few steps away from the door. The leader holds out his gun and fires several shots into the lock.

My father jumps at the sound of the gunshots.

"They're not getting in that way," he says as if trying to calm himself down. "But we do need to move."

He gets up and I follow him as he runs down the hallway in the direction of the staircase sign. We fly down the stairs, stopping three floors down.

"This staircase is secure, and so is the lab, for now," he looks back at me before opening the door, "...the system only gave me a small window."

234

We enter another hallway that looks identical to all of the other ones in this building, just darker. As we run down the hall, the lights activate over us, turning on as we pass.

"This is it!" he yells, out of breath, and grabs me by the arm. He takes out the same keycard as before and scans the lock. He pulls down on the handle, but instead of a click, a red light flashes.

The door is locked.

The door on the opposite end of the hall bursts open with a crash. A group of at least a dozen uniformed men rush out, triggering the motion detected lights over them.

"FREEZE!"

The group of soldiers raise their weapons.

My father frantically swipes the card again.

And again the red light flashes back at us mockingly.

We're stuck.

CHAPTER 53

SURRENDER

The younger version of my father frantically swipes the card again—over and over—each time getting the same results. His shoulders slump over and his arms fall to the side as he gives up.

My eyes bounce from my father to the group of armed men rushing toward us. Their boots shuffle across the floor, loudly squeaking as they approach.

"Put your hands up!" the lead soldier barks.

I look at my dad and watch him raise his hands over his head.

I guess this is where it ends.

Another group, about half as big as the one approaching, file out of the door at the opposite end of the hall.

"Nic!" I hear a voice scream from behind the charging group. "Get down!"

The uniformed group of men turn at the sound of my brother's voice.

Rollins throws something small and dark down the hall, baseball style, reminding me of back when he used to play ball in high school. I remember the time his coach came over for dinner and told my parents how much potential he had—maybe a year or so prior to the night he was arrested and kidnapped by the Government—the night our lives changed forever.

The black ball clinks across the floor about ten or fifteen feet behind the group in the middle of the hallway, and rolls right up to where they have halted. A white cloud of smoke pours from the device and begins to fill the hallway. Gunfire erupts from the opposite end of the hall, followed by screams and the sound of bodies falling to the floor.

The smoke wafts over to where my father and I crouch, burying us. My face is pressed into the ground and my hands are cupped around my ears to block out the loud, echoing gunshots that only seem to be getting closer. My father wraps his arm around the upper part of my back and pulls me toward him.

The shooting stops.

The hallway is quiet again as the white cloud of smoke rises and thins out.

Silence.

I feel the heavy palm of a hand grab the back of my neck, almost picking me right up from the ground.

I tilt my face, ready to see a GA officer towering over me.

But it's Rollins—and Ria and Kingston—along with at least a dozen other teens around the same age that must have all been imprisoned here together. My brother holds a hand out to me and lifts me to my feet.

"We don't have much time," our father says. He pushes himself up and runs his hand across the top of his head. "We need to get into the lab so we can get out of here." His eyes shift from my brother—to the group behind him—to the locked door.

"Don't know how to say thank you?" Rollins raises his voice, releasing some possible built up aggression. He steps toward our father, pushing me to the side as he passes.

"Do you really want to have this argument now? Yes, thank you—thank you for saving us, but if we can't get inside the door, all of this was for nothing."

Rollins reaches into his pocket and pulls out a small plastic card. He holds it between the tips of his thumb and index finger, waving it in front of our father's face.

"This might help."

Dad snatches the card out of my brother's grasp without a word. He spins around and swipes it across the reader. A little green light flashes, clicking the door open.

The lights flicker on as soon as the door opens and we enter the room. Our father dashes across the open floor to the opposite side of the room. He gathers up a pile of papers and folders, stacking them all together in his hands before rushing over to a stack of trays full of test tubes on the counter. He begins emptying the neon red contents of the tubes into a sink built into the middle of the countertop.

I separate myself from the group huddled at the door.

"What're you doing?" I stare over my dad's shoulder already knowing the answer. He's getting rid of the TeleVox vaccine.

He reaches for the final tray full of test tubes when the door flies open behind us.

"Josiah, that's enough!" The loud, booming voice causes my father to freeze in mid-motion.

CHAPTER 54

PRESENT TENSE

"Slowly put down the tray and step away from the counter." Commander Cullen stands at the door guarded by a group of armed men. A pair of FootSoldiers stands at attention in front of the small army. "You're surrounded."

My father stares forward at the bare white wall in front of him, his eyes studying nothing in particular. His hands tighten around the sides of the tray of test tubes. He spins around, holding the tray out in front of his chest. Each test tube is covered by a top, but the red liquid splashes around inside before leveling off.

I follow my father's lead and turn back around toward the door. Every person and drone in the room has a gun except for me and Dad. Two soldiers break away from the commander and disarm the group of prisoners who rescued us. All of them give up their guns willingly, except Kingston and Ria, and of course, my brother.

"You better back up," Rollins says. He pushes the closest soldier in the middle of the chest with the tip of his gun.

The soldier next to him rushes forward and tries to wrestle away the gun from my brother. Two more soldiers abandon the doorway and run over to help.

"Hey!" my father shouts, red-faced and fuming. "Hey! It doesn't matter now anyway."

Cullen takes a couple steps forward, still heavily guarded by his men.

"What are you babbling about, Josiah? *What* doesn't matter?"

Everyone is frozen watching the commander and my father, who still holds the final tray of test tubes.

Dad glances down at the screen on his Receiver. "You're too late. Everything's gone." A smirk begins to grow slowly across his face, matching the rate of the scowl forming on the commander's.

Commander Cullen leans to the side and whispers something into one of his soldier's ear. The soldier then turns around and exits the room.

"Dr. McCready," the commander begins in a more relaxed tone, "what did you do?" He exhales loudly.

The vest under my shirt begins to tremble, vibrating in the center, before trickling outward to my arms. My eyes shoot across the room and find Ria. She stands in front of my brother with her hands held high up over her head. Her eyes darts over at me, her vest is doing the same as mine.

"What I hold in my hand is the last of the TeleVox. All of the electronic records have already been destroyed. Erased."

So that's what he had to do when we separated. My father walks up to me and hands me the tray. I take it with both hands. The entire time my dad does not take his eyes off Commander Cullen. He removes a single test tube from the tray.

240

"This tray is the last of it. When I created this vaccine, I never intended it to be used for evil—for who knows what you and the Government had planned on doing with it."

The vest under my shirt begins to glow. The light grows brighter and brighter until my entire chest looks like it's on fire.

I stare across the room at Ria, Kingston, and Rollins's shirts. All of their vests glow like mine.

"What's going on here?" Commander Cullen shouts in confusion. "What do you have under your shirts?"

My father drops the test tube in his hands as he takes a step back. The glass shatters at his feet spilling the red liquid across the otherwise clean tiled floor.

The soldier in front of my brother flinches and strikes my brother's arm. Rollins shoves the man off of him and knocks Ria to the side.

A gun goes off across the room.

Ria collapses.

I release the tray of test tubes, allowing them to crash to the floor, and run in Ria's direction. I reach out to her just as everything around me goes dark.

EPILOGUE

I spin and thrash around, trying to rip off whatever covers me. The way the material rubs up against my skin makes me picture a heavy wool blanket covering my head. It feels heavier than a blanket though, and it must be long enough to reach the floor because it blocks out all light.

My chest feels like it's on fire.

A sudden, blunt force tackles me, sending me to the ground. I grab the arms of whoever is sitting on top of me, ready to strike the area where its head should be.

"Hold up!" a man's voice yells out, as he struggles to pin both of my arms down.

The wool blanket is pulled off my head to reveal a soldier lying across my chest. He holds his arm underneath my chin and pins me down onto the floor.

"Nicholas! Calm down!"

The crowd of people who gather around me all take a step forward. More than half of them wear a piece of white cloth tied around their bicep with the letter "R" written across it in black.

I blink my eyes and quit struggling, hoping the soldier lets up his grip. My eyes begin to focus on a figure in front of me—Rollins. He's the only one inside of the circle, other than myself and the soldier restraining me. Behind him, Kingston stands with both hands on his knees trying to catch his breath.

The last memory I can recall burns through my mind.

The vest started to activate, right before Ria…

Wait! Where's Ria?

I knock the soldier off of me and jump to my feet. I hold out my hand to send the soldier back, but nothing happens. I begin to feel lightheaded. I start to collapse, but manage to grab onto the closest table and pull myself up the rest of the way. My body feels weak, tired—almost as if my legs are about to give out underneath me at any second. Sweat pours down my face as I spin around. I make eye contact with each person in the room, searching for Ria.

The soldier who was restraining me stands back with both of his hands midway up in the air to protect himself, looking frightened.

I find my brother.

"Where is she?"

Another man runs up behind me and rips the still-warm vest off my chest. He flings it to the side and hugs me. The burning sensation immediately dissipates.

A woman rushes up and grabs both of us, squeezing us together.

"Nicholas! We were so worried about you!" My mother squeezes even harder and kisses me on the side of the head over and over again.

"Mom? Dad?" I pull back. "What's going on? Where am I?

243

Rollins reaches out and puts his hand on the back of my neck. A dark wool blanket hangs off his shoulders. "We're back in our time."

My father releases me and takes a half-step back, but my mother refuses.

"When the Resistance infiltrated the base, one of the first things they did was free me and your mother."

"You both were here the whole time?" I glance around the room. We're in the same building where the NoMads sent us back in time. The Transporter sits on the far side of the room, surrounded by computers. Some have cracked screens and are turned off, but a few remain on.

"The Resistance?" Nothing makes sense to me. My vision is back to normal, but I still feel weak. "Where's Ria?" I force myself stand up, shoulders back, and turn to my brother. "Where is she?"

Rollins looks away.

I find Kingston in the small crowd, but he refuses to make eye contact with me as well.

"Why won't anyone answer me?"

Everyone looks away.

"We have to go back!" I push myself away from the table, but have to catch myself again when my legs almost give out. "We can't just leave her there in the past!"

Rollins reaches out and grabs me.

"We don't have a choice," he whispers in my ear. "Not now. Even if we wanted to return, it wouldn't be safe."

I pull back.

"What do you mean, even if we wanted to?"

"The Transporter was damaged in the battle against the NoMads," Rollins says. This time he makes eye contact with me. "They were barely able to bring us back. Ria's vest must have gotten damaged when she was shot."

"We're going back to get her," I demand.

Rollins exhales and nods his head. "Yes, we'll figure out a way to rescue her. That's what we do."

R. L. MCDANIEL

Born and raised in Florida, R. L. McDaniel currently resides in Tallahassee, Florida, where he has been teaching language arts to middle school students for over ten years. He enjoys playing the guitar and writing in his free time. R. L. McDaniel's published releases include *The Big Hoot* and the *Levitation* series.

To learn more about R. L., please visit...

https://www.RLMcDaniel.com

https://www.instagram.com/RLMcDanielAuthor

Made in the USA
Las Vegas, NV
10 December 2023